RESCUE AT THE ELEVENTH HOUR

By

W. H. G. Kingston

Grace & Truth Books
Sand Springs, Oklahoma

ISBN # 1-58339-122-3
Originally published by the Protestant Truth Society
   of London
Printed by Triangle Press, 1996
Previous printing, Grace & Truth Books, 2003
Current printing, Grace & Truth Books, 2004

Cover design by Ben Gundersen

Grace & Truth Books
3406 Summit Boulevard
Sand Springs, Oklahoma   74063
Phone: 918 245 1500

www.graceandtruthbooks.com
email: gtbooksorders@cs.com

TABLE OF CONTENTS

REMEMBERING THE MARTYRS

The men, the women and the youths, who suffered martyrdom for their faith under the persecuting policy of Mary Tudor, must never be forgotten. Their lives reflect in a wonderful manner how the light of God's truth broke in upon the masses of the British people. It all came about as the result of the great efforts of Wyckliffe and Tyndale to make accessible to the people the Scriptures in their own language.

The eyes of the people being turned to the Scriptures, they saw that the Christian faith was not a priestly one at all, that heaven's throne was approachable direct without earthly mediation, the work of Christ on Calvary was in itself finished and perfect. Thus the mass with its supposed sacrifice and the confessional with its priestly claim of pardoning, were entirely erroneous.

The superstitions of the Middle Ages whereby priestly power had been reinforced became repellent. Images came under the hammer of God's commandments, and were broken down. Purgatory ran entirely contrary to the glorious provision of the gift of Eternal Life through Jesus Christ, so that with Paul men became certain that to be "absent from the body was at once to be at home with the Lord."

All these truths embraced by the heart strengthened every one of the Martyrs to endure the flames and, as Green, the historian, put it, "The terror of death was powerless against men like these."

Chapter 1

THE SCENE AT
THE MARTYRDOM

The morning of the 26th of March 1555 broke dark and lowering: a moral darkness, too, reigned over our now Bible-blessed land of England.

On the previous day, a festival of the Church of Rome had been held, and bareheaded priests in gaudy vestments had paraded the streets of the small town of Brentwood, in Essex, chanting in a foreign tongue, swinging censers, and holding aloft banners with strange devices.

At their head walked a dignitary of their Church, under a silken canopy, bearing in his hand the host—the wafer and the wine, profanely declared to be the real body and blood of the blessed Saviour. There had followed men carrying on their shoulders a wooden image representing the Virgin Mary; for the day was dedicated in the Romish calendar especially to her. And there also came, dragged along on wheels, a figure, which had been brought out on the preceding Monday, of our Lord riding on an ass, when the Jewish people strewed palm leaves before Him, on His entrance into Jerusalem—those who carried, and those who drew the figures believing that by thus toiling they would obtain remission of their sins, while others bowed down and worshipped the figures as they passed.

Another procession, that sad morning of the 26th of March, proceeded through the town of Brentwood. It had set forth from the Swan Inn. There were also priests swinging censers and chanting Latin hymns; and the Sheriff, and Justices, and men-at-arms, and gentlemen on horseback, and servants bearing faggots, and a large and mixed multitude following, of old and young, of farmers, tradesmen, and labourers.

The centre figure, on whom all eyes were fixed, was a young man, fair and slight in stature, whose countenance seemed to beam with joy as he gazed up to heaven and his lips moved in prayer, while every feature was expressive of firm and calm resolution. Anxious, mournful faces looked forth from the windows of the curiously-carved high-roofed houses which lined either side of the broad street; and tears fell from the eyes of many, for that youth was William Hunter, a native of the town through which he was now being led, by the command of cruel and bigoted tyrants, to atone, by a torturing death amid scorching flames, the crime of having right truly loved the Bible.

Knowing in whom he trusted, the young martyr advanced boldly to the stake. It was erected in an open space at the north end of the town; a tall elm tree waved its branches in the fresh air of the morning near the spot. The faggots were piled up—the chain to bind the body was ready. He bade a loving farewell to his aged father. His last act was to throw a book of psalms, so full of comfort to the afflicted, to his brother, who had followed him to the place of execution. A lighted torch was brought; a pardon was offered him if he would recant. Firmly he refused; and entreated all present who loved the Lord Jesus to pray for him.

"Pray for thee! I will no more pray for thee than I would for a dog," exclaimed one of the justices who had come to superintend the execution.

"I pray God this may not be laid to your charge at the last day," said the youth, turning an eye of compassion on his reviler.

The priests, too, taunted him, telling him that the Bible in which he trusted would soon be driven from the land, and no more heard of in the whole world.

"Say, rather that it is the Word of God, it will go forth into all lands, to the uttermost parts of the world; and that, if we refuse it, we do so to our greater condemnation," a voice was heard to say.

In vain was the speaker sought for by the angry justices, that he might explain his meaning. Those words sank into the hearts of some who heard them.

"Lord, have mercy on his soul," cried a gentleman in a compassionate tone. A deep "Amen" burst forth from the crowd; and the priests, seeing that the feeling of the people was against them, set fire to the pile. "Lord, receive my spirit," exclaimed the dying youth. These were his last words. At that moment, the dark clouds, which had hitherto canopied the sky, parted asunder, and the bright sun shone forth gloriously on the scene of death. It was as if a response had come from heaven to assure the multitude that the martyr's prayer was heard, as most certainly it was heard, by the Rewarder of the just who live by faith. The fire was kindled, and soon William Hunter's sufferings were over. He did not die in vain. No true martyr for the cause of Christ does so.

Among the crowd were two young people, Humphrey and Mary Clayton, whose family had not rejected the errors of Rome. They had come, believing that they were performing a meritorious action, to witness the death of the young heretic; or, it might be, in the hope of seeing him recant—for pity even then moved their hearts. Their father was a man of substance, who farmed his own land, situated a mile or so from Brentwood. He was much respected in his neighbourhood as a just man, who gave to all their due—a kind master, and a good father to his family. He lived by the law, and was content with the religion of his forefathers, with the rules of which he found it easy to comply. Slowly the young people bent their steps homeward, when the mourning crowd dispersed. Even those who placed no value on the Bible grieved for the youth whose heroic death they had witnessed.

"Those were strange words we heard just now, about the Bible being the Word of God," said Humphrey to his sister, in a low tone. "If so, methinks those who burn people for reading the book are fighting against God."

"I cannot, at all events, think that the burning of human beings, even though they are heretics, can be pleasant to Him," said Mary, timidly. "But then, surely the great Pope of Rome, and our sovereign lady Queen Mary, must know better than we do about such matters!"

"King Henry, her father, cared little for the Pope; and the late King Edward still less, and favoured the reading of the Bible; and if he was right, Queen Mary and those who support her are wrong," exclaimed Humphrey, raising his voice.

"Hush, hush! dear brother," said Mary; "those are dangerous words to utter, even out here where no one is listening."

"I care not," exclaimed Humphrey impetuously; "I tell thee, dear sister, when I heard that brave lad speak out for the faith he held; when I saw him refuse the offer of life, even when the torch was ready to set fire to the faggots piled around him; when I saw his calm, forgiving spirit; when I heard him pray for his cruel foes; and, firmly trusting in God, remain steadfast to the end, my heart burned within me. I vowed, in spite of the Pope, and the Queen, and Bishop Bonner to boot, to search in that Book he loved so well, to find out what it is which gave him such faith and boldness. If it is truly God's Word, I gain everything by its study; if it is only the work of a man, I risk but my life. Even the Bible's greatest foes dare not to say that it is a device of the evil one.

"No; but they do say that it is a dangerous book for unlearned people to read," said Mary.

"William Hunter was no great scholar, and it brought him that faith, that nobel courage which I would thankfully possess," said Humphrey firmly.

4

"It has brought him to the stake," murmured Mary sorrowfully.

"It brought him a crown of glory and eternal happiness," exclaimed Humphrey. "When the clouds parted, and the sun shone forth gloriously on his head, it seemed as if angels were descending to carry his soul aloft to realms of bliss."

"Oh! dear brother, you think strange things," said Mary affectionately looking at Humphrey; "yet though I possess not your enthusiasm, I will join you in your study of that mysterious Book; and if it brings evil to you, so may it bring it to me likewise."

"Say, rather if it brings faith and hope and joy, a certainty of happiness eternal to me, so may it bring it to you, Mary; and assuredly it will, unless William Hunter trusted in a false friend, and died in vain."

Chapter 2

A DANGEROUS
BUT PRECIOUS BOOK

To obtain a Bible in the sad days of Queen Mary's reign was difficult. To inquire for it publicly was dangerous; still Humphrey Clayton kept to his resolution to possess one. He dared not tell his father, lest he might prohibit him from carrying out his purpose. He had saved some gold pieces—a large sum in those days. Mr. Clayton had business to transact on a certain day with a merchant in London; but, just before, he was laid up with a fit of sickness, and he appointed his steady, thoughtful son, Humphrey, to go in his stead. Humphrey was also to bring out stores for the household. So taking a cart and horse, he joyfully set forth, trusting that now he might accomplish his purpose.

John Harding, the London merchant, kindly received his young guest. His broad brow, clear grey eyes, and the intelligent and kindly expression of his countenance gained him the confidence of all with whom he came in contact. He was known also to be attached to the glorious principles of the Reformation; but, from his cautious conduct, no accusations could be brought against him. He had been abroad for some time; and as Humphrey Clayton came from Brentwood, he inquired the particulars of the execution of William Hunter. Though without himself making any comment, Humphrey told him in a way that brought a satisfied expression into his countenance.

"And you deem that he was unjustly put to death?" he said.

"If for reading and loving the Bible, which he believed to be the Word of God, most unjustly," answered Humphrey firmly.

"And do you read and love the Bible, young man?" asked the merchant, in a kind tone.

"Would that I did," said Humphrey, feeling perfect confidence in the good merchant. "But alas! I do not posses the Book."

"Then you wish for a copy?" said the merchant.

"Indeed I do, and would gladly give these eight gold pieces for one, if money can purchase one," exclaimed Humphrey producing his long-hoarded wealth.

"Put up your purse, young sir," said the merchant kindly. "I will gladly present you with the precious Book, on the condition that you do not let it be known from whom you obtained it. It would be unwise, by bringing myself into trouble, to curtail my power of usefulness. Consider, however, before you accept the gift, that it is dangerous to be found with that book in your possession; and that, through it, the same fate which befell William Hunter may overtake you."

Humphrey's lip curled, and his eye kindled. "If that Book is, as I have been told, the Word of God, a precious gift sent to guide us aright, I fear no danger, so that I may possess it."

"Possess it you shall, dear youth; and may God bless the reading of it to your own soul, and to the souls of those you love," said the merchant warmly.

Humphrey was certain that he had not fallen into a trap, and the merchant felt equally sure that the youth would not betray him. Humphrey then drove off to purchase his provisions; and on his return, some yards of broadcloth, and other articles, were placed in the cart. Among them lay concealed the merchant's priceless gift. With a glad and thankful heart he commenced his homeward journey.

He had been watched by suspicious eyes leaving John Harding's house; and, ere long, as he drove through the city, he was stopped and questioned as to the business he had been about, and the contents of his cart. His answers were clear; and, as for the contents of his cart, the officers were free to examine it. His courage was tried while the officers searched among his goods; but so well had the Bible been concealed that it escaped detection. Once more he entered his cart and drove on.

Unacquainted with the streets of London, he lost his way, and found himself close to an open space surrounded by houses, where a large concourse of people were assembled. He inquired of a passer-by where he was, and for what reason that multitude had collected. Scarcely had he uttered the words, when a column of smoke ascended and flames burst forth from among the crowd.

"Know ye not, young man, that this is Smithfield; and these are pious bishops and lords and other dignitaries and godly men come to burn Master Cardmaker, the late vicar of St. Bride's, and two other defiant and rebellious heretics, a worthy man and his wife, for the love of Christ; and because he first preached and the other two listened to the Gospel. These are happy times, truly." The stranger having thus given vent to his feelings, Humphrey hurried on with a sad countenance.

Humphrey, seeing an open road before him, drove along it, that he might get away from the hateful spot as soon as possible, and at length found himself on the high road leading to Brentwood. His father was well pleased with the way in which he had performed his task. Humphrey would have taken the opportunity of telling him that he had acquired a Bible; but remembering the merchant's caution, he felt that he must wait till another occasion.

In the meantime, he commenced in secret the study of the book; and soon Mary joined him, and became as eager as he was in searching the Scriptures and discovering the inestimable riches therein contained.

Humphrey Clayton had received an excellent education for those days, and was of a peculiarly inquiring mind. About a month after his first visit to London, his father, who was well pleased with the way he had carried out his command, directed him to go again to transact another piece of business with the worthy merchant, John Harding. He was kindly welcomed as before.

"Have you read the Holy Scriptures, and imbibed their truths, young friend?" asked the merchant. "If you have, you will find them like a well of living waters, drinking of which you will never thirst."

"Indeed I have, Master Harding," said Humphrey. "I have found them all that you describe, and more, though now and then I come to difficulties which I should like to have solved. You spoke before of books written in Germany, and by our own Reformers, which show the errors of the Church of Rome, and point out the glorious truths of the Gospel."

"Yes, my young friend, such books do exist in great numbers, even in England. They were written by Tyndale, and Coverdale, by Latimer, Fryth, Bayfield, Cranmer, and many other enlightened Englishmen, while others are translations from works by German, French, and Swiss writers—Drs. Luther and Melancthon, Zwingli, Æcolampadius, Lambert, and others. But you are aware that, even to be found possessed of those books would certainly bring you into great trouble, and that, were it discovered that I had given them to you, the fact would probably bring me to the stake."

"I am well aware of the danger of possessing these books," answered Humphrey, "but I have counted the cost, and am ready to pay it for possessing them, fully believing that they will enlighten my mind, and, with the guidance of the Holy Spirit, lead me to the truth, and enable me to lead others into it."

"Bravely spoken, young man, like a true soldier of Christ," said Master Harding, pressing Humphrey's hand. "If you are ready to fight, I will not shrink from furnishing you with the weapons; and may you use them effectually to the overthrow of ignorance, superstition, and Popish idolatry, and to the establishment of the true faith. I will conceal them as I did your Bible among your goods, and may you reach home with your treasure in safety."

Humphrey again and again thanked the Christian merchant, and asked him for his prayers in addition to his other gifts.

Still, not without anxiety he drove away from John Harding's house. He could not help fancying that the object of his visit might have been suspect. He could honestly say that he had been sent to transact business with Master John Harding, by his father, a well-known Catholic gentleman near Brentwood. Yet if the officers of the Government were to examine his goods and discover the books, he should implicate, not only the merchant, but his father also. More than once, as he drove slowly along, he thought that he saw people watching him.

He passed two or three melancholy groups. Two young women, and their aged mother, were being dragged off to prison on a charge of heresy, while young ruffians in the street were insulting them and reminding them of their probable fate at the stake. Another group came along, with countenances denoting grief, horror, and indignation also. One bore a hat, another a stick, and a third a cloak. These things were all that remained to them on earth of the father and guide of their youth, who that morning had been burned at Smithfield. Humphrey did not breathe freely till he got into the open country, and was able to quicken the speed of his horse. He again reached home safely, and lost no time in beginning the study of the works of which he had become possessed. His sister Mary joined him in his studies, and fully consumed the principles of the Reformation.

Chapter 3

WHAT THAT BOOK REVEALS

Both Humphrey and Mary honoured and loved their father. Should they keep back from him the glorious truth they had discovered—every day becoming more precious to their own souls? No, they would tell him how they had been employed, and entreat him to read and search the blessed book with them. One evening, as they all three sat together, the servants having retired from the hall, Humphrey went out, and returned, bringing back the Bible in his hands.

"Father," he said, "I have to entreat your pardon for concealing from you what I have been about; and also, I beg you not to inquire how this book came into my possession. I have found in it all that its strongest advocates assert that it possesses, and I would that you also would search and judge whether I praise it more than it deserves."

Mr. Clayton looked at his son with an expression of anxiety in his countenance, beaming at the same time with the fondest affection.

"But this study may bring you into trouble, dear boy," he remarked.

"If the book is of God, of which I am well assured, it will take me out of it triumphantly," answered Humphrey. "Oh, father, dear father, read it," he added warmly.

Mary echoed his words.

"Or let me read it to you," continued Humphrey. "In this book we have explained numberless subjects which have long seemed to me deep and unfathomable mysteries; I never could understand, till I read the Bible, how sin entered into the world, and how sin and its consequences were to be got rid of."

"Why, my dear son, surely, as the Church tells us, by penance and good works, and the prayers of the saints," said Mr. Clayton, calmly.

"Oh, no, no," cried Humphrey. "The Gospel tells us that good works can only proceed from faith in Christ and love to Him—that it is repentance, not penance, that God requires. Not a word does it say about the prayers of saints. But there is one verse that, in a few words, explains the whole subject. It is in St. Paul's first epistle to the Corinthians, 15th chapter and 22nd verse: 'As in Adam all die, even so in Christ shall all be made alive.' In other words, as by the disobedience of Adam, all his descendants became sinful; so by the obedience of Christ, who offered Himself up as a sacrifice to an offended God, shall all who trust in Him be freed from their sin, and be presented holy ever and ever; and by this way, and by this alone, can they be saved."

"But, surely, my son, if we have committed sin, it is necessary to perform penance to get rid of sin; and if we cannot pray properly by reason of our sin, surely God will hear the prayers of the saints, who are with Him, if we ask them to intercede for us," persisted Mr. Clayton. "Then, if we are sinful, it would be wrong, as the priests say it is, for us laymen to drink the blood of Christ; and, again, surely a loving mother, like the blessed Virgin Mary, will be ready to hear our prayers, and her Son will be more willing to receive them through her, than direct from us sinful creatures! Once more, if we are sinful, how necessary it must be to have a place like purgatory, where we can be cleansed from our sins. Does not it show the mercy of God that He allows the prayers and offerings of faithful believers offered in masses to shorten the stay of souls in that place of purification and punishment? We must acknowledge that there are mysteries; and surely, that of transubstantiation is a great one; but is it the less to be believed?

"The Holy Scriptures, too, are full of difficulties; and surely, therefore, it must be dangerous for unlearned people to read them. We should be grateful to our Holy Mother Church, and the ancient fathers, to interpret them for us, and to give us such portions as may prove to our edification. Once more, how useful are images, and pictures, and ceremonies, and music, and incense to keep alive our faith, and symbolize its mysteries. How can we dare to say, that when a saint sees an image of himself set up, his blessed spirit does not descend to dwell in that image, that he may the more readily hear the prayers offered to him? To prove, also, his powers, will he not naturally work miracles, if God thinks fit to allow him the privilege?

"Surely too, it is important that there should be unity among Christians; and how can unity be maintained, without one great head, like our Holy Father, the Pope? And for the same reason, how important it is that he should be infallible; and how satisfactory to feel that, in the true Church, we have a sure and safe guide; and that we need give ourselves no further concern as to matters of faith, with such a rule as she affords us. Oh! how satisfactory, too, that we are able to go and confess our sins to a good priest, who, being a man like ourselves, can hear us patiently, and has the authority of the Holy Church to absolve us.

"Equally satisfactory, almost, is it to know that, by labouring in good works, we may merit the favour of God; and also that if, by our honest toil and industry, we can save up money, we may purchase indulgences from our Holy Father, the Pope, and save our own souls from years of torment in purgatory, and also the souls of those we have loved on earth, or even those in whom we have been in any way interested. Then, my dear son, let us be thankful that we are children of the Holy Apostolic infallible Mother Church, beyond whose pale all must, of necessity, not having the advantages we possess, be condemned for ever; and do not let us, by prying into the mysteries of the Scriptures, or by otherwise infringing any of her rules, run the risk of being outside that pale, and being lost for ever, with the heathen and heretics."

Mr. Clayton spoke the sentiments of an honest, conscientious Papist, who had not troubled himself by looking deeply into religious matters, and was content to abide, without questioning, by the faith in which he had been brought up. One thing had, however, startled him—the burning of heretics, of which he had heard on the Continent, and which had taken place in Henry the Eighth's reign in England. It was very troubling that the burnings had now been begun again under the sanction of Queen Mary. He was a kind-hearted man, and his heart had revolted against these cruelties; but, believing that the Church of Rome was infallible, and knowing that she sanctioned them, he had begun to persuade himself that his heart and judgment were at fault, and that it was from weakness and want of faith that he saw them in the light he did.

Still, more than once, he said to himself; "No; surely God cannot like to see His creatures burned. He made this world beautiful, and, I doubt not, good; and He has given loving, gentle hearts to some people. I know He did to my dear wife, and she wept bitterly when she heard of those burnings; and often she read Wycliffe's Bible, till fear of the consequences made me steal it away from her, and sink it to the bottom of our horse-pond—as, for her sake, I could not bring myself to burn it."

Such was Reginald Clayton's thoughts; yet he was no bigot. He believed that he had made an answer to his son's request, and so strongly put forth all the claims of the Church of Rome that it would not be repeated.

Humphrey did not reply hastily. He first earnestly prayed that the Holy Spirit would enlighten his mind, and put such arguments into his mouth, that he might be able to reply convincingly to his father's arguments. Mary, too, was earnestly praying that the light might beam forth on her father's mind, so that he might be led into all truth. Humphrey was seated on a low stool, with the Bible on his knees—

"Dear father," he said, after some time looking up, "you believe in the Holy Spirit?"

"Certainly," said Mr. Clayton.

"And that His object is to teach us of the things of God and to guide us into all truth," said Humphrey.

"How do we know that?" asked Mr. Clayton. "I thought that the Church would guide us into all truth."

"Father, that body of persons which has assumed to be the Church, and has been called the Church, has led us all into error by keeping from us the Holy Scriptures, and by denying the teaching of the Holy Spirit. See here, father, in the 14th chapter of John, 26th verse: 'But the Comforter, which is the Holy Ghost, whom the Father will send in my name, he shall teach you all things, and bring all things to your remembrance, whatsoever I have said unto you.' Again, in the 16th chapter and 13th verse: 'Howbeit when he, the Spirit of truth, is come, he will guide you into all truth.' Also I find in the 15th chapter, 26th verse: 'But when the Comforter is come, whom I will send unto you from the Father, even the Spirit of truth, which proceedeth from the Father, he shall testify of me.'

"In the 2nd chapter of the Acts, we are told how fully the promise was fulfilled—how this mighty event took place; and, vast multitudes of people of all nations being collected together, the Holy Spirit, in the form of cloven tongues of fire, did actually descend, and sat on each believer present, thus showing, by a visible sign, that there might be no doubt or mistake of the Divine influence which had entered into each of them. The blessed Lord promised that He would then be with all believers, then also with us, even unto the end of the world. Then, dear father, believing this, let us kneel down and pray that the Holy Spirit may be sent to guide us into all truth, being assured that He will without fail be sent to us."

Mr. Clayton bowed his head; and the three, he and his two children, knelt down, and trustingly, and yet humbly, prayed that the Holy Spirit might be sent to guide them into all truth.

"Dear father, may I now show you how the Church of Rome is contrary, in numerous important points, to the Holy Scriptures, and, therefore, not only not rightly called the true Church, but unworthy to be called a Christian Church at all?"

"Yes, let me hear," said Mr. Clayton, meekly.

"I will be brief, then, father, and enlarge afterwards on the more important points," said Humphrey. "First, we must understand that God is a pure, holy, loving, merciful, and just God, that He delights in mercy and forgiveness, and that no human love can equal His love for the creatures He has formed. Still He thought fit to make man, created pure and holy, a free agent—to choose the good or the evil. Why evil existed is a mystery we cannot fathom. Man chose the evil, and then all his descendants became evil, and prone to sin, and subject to death. Yet, at once, God, in His mercy, formed a plan by which man might escape the consequences of sin, and triumph over death. It was that His Son—part of Himself, who had been with Him from the beginning—should be born into the world by a woman, and should be sacrificed for the sins of mankind. It was a wonderful plan; so wonderful, that people, unless taught of the Spirit, cannot comprehend it.

"He chose a certain people, the Jews, on whom He imposed the performance of certain rites and ceremonies, both to keep alive a remembrance of His beneficent promise, and that they might comprehend clearly the object of the intended mighty sacrifice. The object and nature of this glorious sacrifice was, however, not understood by the stiff-necked among them; nor by the Greek philosophers; nor was the mode by which its benefits were to be obtained. It is not, alas! understood at the present day by numbers and numbers who call themselves Christians.

"In the first place, it was a complete, entire, perfect work. On account of its very simplicity and perfectness, it was not understood; neither, for the same reason, were the means by which its full benefits are to be obtained comprehended. The moment Christ's blood was shed on Calvary, and He had uttered the awful words, 'It is finished,' and yielded up the ghost—that moment the work of salvation was freely, fully accomplished; neither angels, nor saints in heaven, nor men on earth, could do more to save man from the consequences of sin, from eternal damnation. All types, ceremonies, and sacrifices had come to an end, were of no further avail.

"Jesus' great sacrifice was received for the sins of all the world, and its benefits offered, by grace, to man freely, fully, without price. No penance, no works, no labours were required. Two things only were required—man was to feel and acknowledge that he was sinful, not to man, but to God, and to repent of his sins; and then to put faith in Christ's blood, to believe that his sins were washed away by that blood; that a merciful, pure, and holy God would receive him, thus made pure and holy, by which God ordained that man could be saved.

"There is an account in the Old Testament of an event which occurred when the Israelites were wandering in the desert. As a punishment for their disobedience, serpents were sent among them, whose fiery bite caused horrible suffering, and certain and speedy death. Moses was ordered by God to make a brazen serpent, the emblem of healing among the Egyptians, and to prove the faith of the people; they were told that if they would but look on it, they should be healed. Numbers did look on it and were instantly healed; they did nothing else, they paid no price, they simply looked, repented of their sin, desiring to be healed.

"How our Lord Himself refers to this circumstance to explain the object of His intended sacrifice, and the mode by which its benefits were to be obtained, see here in the 3rd

chapter of St. John, beginning at the 14th verse: 'And as
Moses lifted up the serpent in the wilderness, even so must
the Son of man be lifted up: That whosoever believeth in him
should not perish, but have eternal life.' John 3:16 says, 'For
God so loved the world, that he gave his only begotten Son,
that whosoever believeth in him should not perish, but have
everlasting life. For God sent not his Son into the world to
condemn the world; but that the world through him might be
saved.'

"Here is nothing, dear father, about penances, or
purgatory, or indulgences, or confession to a priest, or
absolution, or invocation of saints, or the sacrifice of the
mass, or transubstantiation, or the Church, or the infallibility
of this or that Church, or baptism in this or that form, or
ceremonials, or works. Oh! No, no! Our Lord says it Himself,
and repeats it, 'that whosoever believeth in him should not
perish, but have everlasting life.' That is the great, the
important thing that saved the thief on the cross.

"There is another thing needful, as our Lord had just
before explained to Nicodemus, Repentance—an earnest
desire to be saved—to live with God: (John 3:3, 5) 'Jesus
answered and said unto him, Verily, verily, I say unto thee,
Except a man be born again, he cannot see the kingdom of
God.... Jesus answered, Verily, verily, I say unto thee, except
a man be born of water and of the Spirit, he cannot enter into
the kingdom of God.' That is to say he must put away the old
man of sin, the evil spirit of the world, which has hitherto
ruled in him, and submit to the guidance of the Holy Spirit.

"We know not how that Holy Spirit comes, but He
does come; as our Lord says, (John 3:8) 'The wind bloweth
where it listeth, and thou hearest the sound thereof, but canst
not tell whence it cometh, and whither it goeth: so is every
one that is born of the Spirit.' I might produce text upon text,
and line upon line, to show how utterly at variance the Papal
System is with that which Christ established while on earth;
how utterly senseless and useless, or worse than useless, are

20

all forms and ceremonies. Unless a man is born again of the Spirit—unless he repents and trusts to the blood of Jesus alone, and to nothing else, to wash away his sins, and thus to make him acceptable to the Father, I say that forms and ceremonies are worse than useless, because they only deceive and mislead. Unless the change of heart is real—unless the Spirit is there; then certain forms and certain ceremonies may be useful and convenient, but they are nothing more; there can be no saving power in them, or we detract from the merits of Christ's perfect work."

"What! No use in good works?" suddenly exclaimed Mr. Clayton, interrupting his son. "Christ set us the example, merely by performing many good works."

"Yes, truly, father; He performed numberless works of love, and charity, and kindness; He called people to repent; He preached, He taught, He exhorted, He rebuked; but He nowhere says, Do these things that ye may be saved. One of His objects in coming on earth was to set us an example how to live; and to show how happiness, lost by Adam's transgression, might once more be enjoyed, even on earth. I find verse upon verse, or rather chapter upon chapter, in St. Paul's epistles, to prove that man is not saved by works, but by faith and grace.

"To the Galatians, he says, 2nd chapter, 16th verse: 'Knowing that a man is not justified by the works of the law, but by the faith of Jesus Christ, even we have believed in Jesus Christ, that we might be justified by the faith of Christ, and not by the works of the law: for by the works of the law shall no flesh be justified.' Again, to the Ephesians, he says, 2nd chapter, 4th to 9th verses, and what glorious words are they! 'But God, who is rich in mercy, for his great love wherewith he loved us. Even when we were dead in sins, hath quickened us together with Christ, (by grace ye are saved;) And hath raised us up together, and made us sit together in heavenly places in Christ Jesus: That in the ages to come he might shew the exceeding riches of his grace in his kindness

21

toward us through Christ Jesus. For by grace are ye saved through faith; and that not of yourselves: it is the gift of God: Not of works, lest any man should boast.'

"But, to correct any misconception of this important truth, St. James, in his general epistle, says, 1st chapter 22nd verse: 'But be ye doers of the word, and not hearers only, deceiving your own selves.' Again, 2nd chapter, 17th and 18th verses: 'Even so faith, if it hath not works, is dead, being alone. Yea, a man may say, Thou hast faith, and I have works: shew me thy faith without thy works, and I will shew thee my faith by my works.' The 20th verse: 'But wilt thou know, O vain man, that faith without works is dead?'

"It is not works, then, however excellent, that save us. Christ has done the work that saves us; but we are called upon to repent, believe, and prove our belief by our love and desire to please Him, our gracious Saviour, by imitating, as far as we have the power, those works of charity and kindness to our fellow-creatures, of which He sets us an example; and, I may also add, obedience to God's will and prayers to Him."

"I see, I see!" exclaimed Mr. Clayton; "Christ's great sacrifice saves us completely—entirely. Everything else we can do is simply to prove our faith, and love, and gratitude."

Chapter 4

HISTORY'S HAMMER

Another evening, Mr. Clayton and his children were seated together.

"I will now, dear father," said Humphrey, "go over the tenets of the Church of Rome, which the Protestant divines and doctors consider gross errors. Before, however, I do so, I will take a glance at the religious condition of the civilized world up to the time that the Church of Rome began to gain influence and power. The lower classes were generally gross Pagans, or poor wandering Jews, driven out of their own country, yet clinging to their ceremonies and their law. The upper, or educated classes, were philosophers from Egypt, Greece, Persia, and other parts of the East, holding many different doctrines, more or less adverse to the spirit of Christianity—most of them diametrically opposed to it.

"The Christians also had greatly increased in numbers and influence, and churches had been established in all directions; but already numerous schisms and heresies had sprung up, and ten bloody persecutions had tried the faith of all. In Rome, it may be affirmed that the true and primitive Church had almost been driven underground, and lay hid in the catacombs. When, however, Constantine declared himself a Christian, and resolved to support the Christians, affairs were changed. The Pagan priests had hitherto reigned supreme, and kept the minds of the people in subjection. They used their oracles, their gorgeous ceremonies, their rich dresses and processions, their fables and lying wonders of all sorts. These Pagan priests saw that their day of power was over, unless they could themselves take a lead in the form of worship prescribed by the Emperor. Some possibly were real converts to Christianity, but the greater number became nominal Christians for the sake of the worldly place and power at once commenced in the Church at Rome, utterly unbecoming the character of Christianity.

"No sooner, indeed, had the apostate Emperor Julian come to the throne, than these pretended Christian priests showed themselves perfectly ready to re-establish, with greater splendour than before, all the rites and ceremonies of Paganism. Directly the Emperor was dead, they as readily again professed themselves Christians. Many Jews also probably found it to their interest to profess Christianity; some undoubtedly, had been originally really converted.

"No wonder, then, that many Pagan, and some Jewish ceremonies and rites and observances were introduced into the so-called Christian Church at Rome. Whatever was likely to please the taste of the upper classes, and attract the idolaters among the lower orders, was speedily made a part of the new public worship. The idols, the statues of their old divines, were transformed into saints and martyrs; their shrines were dedicated to the new worship; the temples were freshly named; and every object connected with Pagan worship, which could be of use in tempting the Pagans to profess the new faith, with much ingenuity was adapted to suit the worship of this so-called Christian Church.

"Hitherto, one of the modes of trying the faith of persons accused of Christianity, was to make them burn incense to the gods. Incense was now introduced into the service of this Church. A basin of water was placed at the entrance of many temples, that the worshippers might sprinkle themselves; one was placed for a similar purpose at the doors of the churches. Lamps had in many temples been kept ever burning, and candles at mid-day had occasionally been placed lighted on the altars, though the idea had been ridiculed by some of the Pagan writers as absurd. It had ever been the custom of the worshipers of the sun to turn to the east, and to the rising of the luminary of the day. Their priests at Rome introduced the same custom, and the Christians were told that they bowed towards the east because Jerusalem was in that direction.

"In Egypt, and many parts of the East, Pagan monks had long existed, who separated themselves from the world, and inflicted all sorts of tortures on their bodies, under the idea that by such means they could please the malign deities whom they ignorantly worshipped. Vestal virgins and begging priest had long existed; all these classes were soon established in the new Romish Church under the name of nuns and friars, and monks and hermits. The Egyptian priests had their heads shaved; the new Romish priests and monks and friars, in most instances having theirs shaved, kept them so, and the custom became general. It had for ages been the practice to make votive offerings at the shines of the gods, greatly to the benefit of the priests who presided at them; the pretended Christian priests were not likely to allow so lucrative a custom to be abandoned, and therefore rigidly kept it up from the first. Indeed, when we consider how strong a hold idolatry had of the minds of the people, and how deeply rooted it was in the affections, we cannot be surprised that such should have been the case; though we must regret that, in the struggle between Paganism and Christianity, Paganism should in Rome have been triumphant and able to strangle Christianity, as it most effectually and assuredly did.

"Even then there were some real Christians in that so-called Christian Church; some might have occasionally been raised to rank and dignity, although the idolaters, or rather the Atheists (for such were the persons possessed of any real influence), took good care that they should have no power to alter the system they had established. One thing is very certain, that the Christian Church established by St. Paul, when residing in his own hired house had totally disappeared from Rome before the close of the sixth century, if not rather at a much earlier period.

"Gradually, the Atheists gained more and more influence, and the professors of primitive Christianity were driven away from the seven-hilled city to dwell in mountain regions or distant lands; and among others, to Britain, where I believe, the light of truth has never been totally extinguished.

"In the first six centuries, the Bishops of Rome had no jurisdiction beyond the limits of their immediate diocese; and this is evident from the fact that, in the first general Council, held at Nice, 325, summoned by the Emperor, the Bishops of Alexandria and Antioch were declared to have according to custom, the same authority over the churches subordinate to them that the Bishops of Rome had over those that lay about that city; and that, in the sixth century, when John, the Bishop of Constantinople, assumed to himself the title of universal bishop, Pelagius II, and Gregory I, both Bishops of Rome, protested against him in the strongest language; the latter winding up his arguments with these remarkable words:—'I indeed confidently assert that whosoever calls himself, or desires to be called "Universal Priest," that person, in his vain elation, is the precursor of Antichrist; because, through his pride, he exalts himself above the others.' Yet, this was the very thing that the successors of Gregory were about most completely to do.

"Although the title Pope, derived from the Greek papa, and signifying father, was originally taken by all bishops, it was not till the end of the eleventh century that Gregory VII in a Council held at Rome, ordered that the title should be given exclusively to the Bishop of Rome. Those bishops had already well merited the condemnation pronounced on them by the first Gregory. Among the Popes there were already, to be followed by several others, some of the most infamous and detestable characters that have ever disgraced humanity. The names of Alexander III, Julius III, Gregory VII, John XVIII, Urban VI, Julius II, Alexander VI, and Benedict IX, will ever remain in history as proofs of the awful extent of villainy and crime of which man is capable. I need not enter more into that subject. Such is the information I have gleaned from books written by earnest men, whose great anxiety and prayer has been to ascertain the truth, and put it forth for the benefit of their fellow men.

"If we are to judge a Church by her fruits, by the vices of her rulers, her bishops and priests, by the character of the laity attached to her, how can we do otherwise than condemn the Church of Rome, and cry out to our friends, 'Come out of her; and partake not longer of her abominations.'"

Mr. Clayton cast a look of astonishment and dismay at his son. He could only say, "Alas! Are these things so? How long, then, have I been misguided and deceived?"

"Indeed, dear father, they are true, I fully believe," answered Humphrey. "But it may be satisfactory to you to try each doctrine of the Church of Rome by the doctrine taught in the blessed Gospel, and see how far the two agree. I have been doing so for many months, and with the aid of certain books—some written in Germany, others by Protestants in England; and I have come to the conclusion the doctrines of the Romish Church are totally at variance with the Gospel, and clearly exhibit their Pagan origin."

"My son, I am sure that you have been earnestly seeking the truth; and I am equally sure that the Holy Spirit, whose guidance you have sought, will lead you and me into it," said Mr. Clayton solemnly, "therefore, let us go on without fear, confident that if Rome is right, we shall be led back to her, but that if wrong, we shall receive the truth as it is in the Gospel, and the Gospel alone, and have knowledge, strength, and courage, to protest against her errors and impositions."

"Well then, father, I will without delay go over the chief points against which those who love the Bible protest," said Humphrey, drawing some pamphlets from his pockets, and a paper of manuscript notes. "First, then, about this Church of Rome, which professes to have been founded by St. Peter, and to be the mother of all Churches. There is no proof whatever that St. Peter ever was at Rome, but rather that he never was there; and, certainly, the Christian Church there was founded by St. Paul, when he lived in his own hired house. If there could have been a mother Church, it must have been the Church at Jerusalem, founded by Christ Himself and His disciples.

"The Church, however, clearly means the spiritual Church, of which Christ is the head corner-stone, composed of all faithful believers in the all-sufficient sacrifice He made of Himself, being the Son of God. No Church can claim to be the mistress of others, for the believing Gentiles were to be fellow-heirs with the believing Jews—to be of the same body, and to possess the same privileges. The Pope's assumption of power is blasphemous, and in direct violation of the prerogatives of the Lord Jesus Christ, who is Head over all things to His Church—Ephesians 1:22; 4:15; Colossians 1:18; 2:19.

"For the first six centuries, indeed, the Bishops of Rome, though called Papas or Popes, as were numerous other bishops at the same time, and all the bishops in the East had no jurisdiction beyond the limits of their own immediate diocese; and it was not till the end of the eleventh century that Gregory VII, in a Council held at Rome, ordered that the title should be given exclusively to the Bishop of Rome. This I have before stated; but it cannot be too often repeated, with regard to the infallibility of the Church of Rome, not to speak of the infamous lives of numbers of the Popes and Cardinals, that Councils have constantly contradicted each other; that she has taught doctrines that were not only not supported by, but contrary to the Holy Scriptures; that there have been several rival Popes at the same time, each claiming to be infallible, each asserting different opinions and denouncing their opponents as infamous.

"Had the Church of Rome been infallible, St. Paul would not have addressed to that Church, which he himself founded (and surely if it was ever pure and infallible, it was at the time)—I say he would not have addressed these

28

remarkable words: (Romans 11:18-22) 'Boast not against the branches. But if thou boast, thou bearest not the root, but the root thee. Thou wilt say then, the branches were broken off, that I might be grafted in. Well, because of unbelief they were broken off, and thou standest by faith. Be not high-minded, but fear: For if God spared not the natural branches, take heed lest he also spare not thee. Behold therefore the goodness and severity of God: on them which fell, severity; but toward thee, goodness, if thou continue in his goodness: otherwise thou also shalt be cut off.'

"Did the Church at Rome continue pure and holy, worshipping God in sincerity and truth? Numbers of Romish writers even, confess that she did not. History loudly proclaims her follies, her sins, and abominations. The most respectable of the Popes were those chosen by the Emperors—who found that they could not trust the Cardinal Bishops and Priests to elect their Chief Pontiff—Pontifex Maximus. The celebrated Hildebrand, Gregory VII, at length, in the eleventh century, got his foot on the necks of Emperors and Kings, his example being imitated and his system being carried out still more practically by Innocent III, in the thirteenth century.

"Now, it is very certain, from what I have said, and from what I have read, that one of two things have happened: either the Christian Church in Rome was cut off, or Paul was made a liar! Papal supremacy, of course, falls, if what I have already advanced, is true. The Pope says that he derives authority over all Christians from Peter, because Peter was first Bishop of Rome. There is no proof that Peter was Bishop of Rome. Peter himself was not superior to the other apostles; nor are the Popes, even if they are his successors, which they are not. Besides, Christ is the only supreme Head of the Church, and its unity consists in its recognizing Him as its living and only Head.

"When our Lord addressed Peter with the words, 'Thou art Peter, and upon this rock I will build my Church,'

Peter had, just before, declared his belief in the Messiahship of our Lord; replying to Christ's question, 'Whom say ye that I am?' 'Thou art the Christ, the Son of the living God.' Then our Lord says: 'On this confession of the truth, which you, Peter, have made, I will build my Church;' that is to say, let it be the fundamental principle in the belief of all who call themselves Christians. This is what you are to preach when you go forth to proclaim the Gospel. And He immediately afterwards explained to His disciples how He—the Son of God, as He had declared Himself—must be sacrificed and raised again the third day.

"Peter, who was evidently far from enlightened on all points, attempted to persuade our Lord to avoid the sacrifice of Himself; Christ turned round to Peter, whom the Romanists declare had just been made head of the Church, and said in Matthew 16:23, 'But he turned, and said unto Peter, Get thee behind me, Satan: thou art an offence unto me: for thou savourest not the things that be of God, but those that be of men.'

"It was not, indeed, till the day of Pentecost that Peter became wholly converted and enlightened; and then, indeed, the keys or knowledge necessary to teach men how they might enter the kingdom of heaven were committed to him, as they were to the other apostles; and the kingdom of heaven, it must be understood, is Christ's kingdom here on earth. All believers are subjects of that kingdom; and unless a person enters it here, he will never enter it at all.

"But really, my dear father, it seems to me that the whole ground has been swept away from under the feet of the Papists, from what I have already said. They support the worship of images, by referring to Exodus 25:18, where Moses is commanded to make two cherubim, and to place them over the mercy seat; and to Numbers 21:8, where he was commanded to make a brazen serpent. Not a word, however, in either account, is said about worshipping these devices; but numberless passages occur throughout Scripture where anything like the worship of images is most strictly prohibited, besides in the commandments.

"Nothing can be stronger than our Lord's own words, to prevent anything like adoration offered to the Virgin Mary. The worship paid to her in Rome is clearly derived from, and a mixture of, that paid to Diana, the great goddess of the Ephesians, and to Juno; and it is remarkable that the peacock's tails carried before the Pope, when, in the ceremonies of the Church, he is carried about on men's shoulders, are the special insignia of Juno, the Queen of Heaven—the same name given to the Virgin Mary.

"As to Invocation of Saints, not a line in Scripture supports it; but, on the contrary, St. Paul says, 'For we have not an high priest which cannot he touched with the feeling of our infirmities; but was in all points tempted like as we are, yet without sin. Let us therefore come boldly unto the throne of grace, that we may obtain mercy, and find grace to help in time of need' (Hebrews 4:15, 16). Our Lord Himself says, 'Come unto me, all ye that labour and are heavy laden, and I will give you rest' (Matthew 11:28). Then, are we not insulting Christ when we refuse to accept this merciful, loving, kind invitation, and refuse to go direct to Him, and tell Him of all our wants—our sorrows—to confess to Him all our sins? Surely we are!

"Oh! What a kind, loving, merciful heart has Jesus! No human love can equal it; not that, even, of His virgin mother; through whom He was born in the flesh that He might feel for us. Not by one single word does He ever show that He desired any special respect paid to His mother, though she was assuredly blessed in being selected for the honour of bearing Him.

"As also we have a great High Priest in the heavens, all earthly priesthoods were abolished; we are to confess our sins to our loving Saviour; and, therefore, it is blasphemous presumption in a man to listen to a confession of sins, and faithless, ignorant folly in those who so confess. The forgiveness of sins belongs to God alone, and He has refused to award it, unless to those trusting in the precious blood of His Son alone. The apostles even were only directed to assure those who did thus trust in Christ's atonement that they were absolved. Every believer has this assurance, or ought to have it, and the minister can do no more than remind him of it. Therefore, every time the Pope or one of his priests pronounces absolution as a judge, and by way of jurisdiction, he is guilty of gross blasphemy.

"But I must once more speak of the love of Christ, to show that those who pray to any other than to Him, are guilty of gross ingratitude—of rebellion and insult to that love. What should we think of a child, who, turning from a kind father who had promised to give him everything he asked, persisted in going to a stranger for what he wanted?

"Yet, of all the blasphemies and insults to Christ of which the Church of Rome is guilty, the greatest, perhaps is that of offering up the Mass—or the sacrifice of the Mass, as it is called—for which the dogma of Transubstantiation was invented, in the eighth century. I repeat, dear father that I look upon the sacrifice of the Mass as the crowning impiety and blasphemy of the Papists. Every time it is offered up, Christ, who sits on high at the right hand of God, our advocate with the Father, pleading the all-sufficient merit of His blood, shed on Calvary, is insulted and blasphemed. The question at issue is this: Did Jesus Christ die on the cross, and is His death a sufficient and complete sacrifice for the sins of mankind? If so, no other sacrifice can possibly be needed. We have to study every passage we meet with Scripture bearing on the subject.

"The most important passage is that in which Christ first instituted the communion (Matthew 26:26-28); 'And as they were eating, Jesus took bread, and blessed it, and brake it, and gave it to the disciples, and said, Take, eat; this is my body. And he took the cup, and gave thanks, and gave it to them, saying, Drink ye all of it; for this is my blood of the new testament, which is shed for many for the remission of sins. Or, in other words, this wine represents My blood, which is about to be shed for the remission, or absolution, of the sins of as many as believe in Me.'

"This figurative language is employed frequently in the Bible; (Luke 8:11) 'Now the parable is this: The seed is (represents) the word of God.' (John 10:7), 'Then said Jesus unto them again, Verily, verily, I say unto you, I am the door of the sheep'—or, I represent the door; (John 15:1), 'I am the true vine'—or, I am represented by the vine; and, again (1 Corinthians 10:4), 'That rock was Christ,' or represented Christ—otherwise Christ would be a door, a vine, and a rock at the same time. Then, again, the communion was instituted immediately after the Passover, which it was to supersede, and which was especially a commemorative ceremony.

"Again, directly after Christ had pronounced these words, and distributed the bread and wine, He expressly calls the latter 'the fruit of the vine,' thereby showing that no change of substance had taken place. In every instance recorded in the Scriptures, when one substance is changed into another, the change is plainly stated, so that those present had evidence of it. Thus the ruler of the feast in Cana of Galilee tasted the wine, and he knew it was wine. Our Lord says, 'This do ye in remembrance of Me;' but not a word does He speak about a sacrifice. Remembrance, of necessity, implies the bodily absence of Christ whenever this communion is celebrated by His people, though He promises to be present in the spirit on that occasion (though not in the bread and wine), as on all other occasions where two or three of His disciples are gathered together.

"Lastly, in the Primitive Church, in the time of the apostles—and by that alone should we look for guidance in any custom—the celebration of the communion is expressly described as 'breaking of bread.' Also, it is clear, from the language of St. Paul to the Corinthians (1 Corinthians 11:26), 'For as often as ye eat this bread, and drink this cup, ye do shew the Lord's death till he comes.' What more implicit statement—what more clear language can be required? We eat the actual bread, we drink the actual wine, to commemorate the Lord's death—to remind us of it—to prove that we trust in it—because He is absent in the body, though we by faith, know that He, in spirit, is in the midst of us. This we are required to do till He comes in His glorified body. Then faith will be no more required, because we shall see Him as His is.

"Once more, in the discourse on the establishment of the communion, our Lord speaks of Himself as bread, and not of the bread as His body. If this was to be taken literally, it would prove that His body was changed into bread—but certainly not that a loaf of bread, or a wafer, could be changed into His body. Eating His flesh, and drinking His blood, of course means 'believing' on Him, taking Him in spiritually as we eat bread and drink wine. Here is another argument against Transubstantiation, or any dogma like it. When Jesus—having fed five thousand in a miraculous way on bread and fish, as recorded in John 6:26—says, in verse 51, 'I am the living bread which came down from heaven,' if He spoke in a literal sense of His flesh, it would prove that His human nature came down from heaven, which is contrary to fact.

"However, if this passage does prove Transubstantiation, as the Papists assert, then the declaration—in verse 54 of John, chapter 6, 'Who so eateth my flesh, and drinketh my blood, hath eternal life'—would prove that every one who receives the sacrament in the Church of Rome must be saved; but the declaration, in verse 53—'Except ye eat the flesh of the Son of man, and drink his blood, ye have no life in you'— would also prove that no one can be saved unless he receive the communion in both kinds. Now, as the Church of Rome only administers it in one kind to the laity, it follows that only the clergy can be saved, and that all laymen must be damned."

"Enough, enough, my son!" exclaimed Mr. Clayton. "How have my eyes and my understanding been blinded? As I have listened to you, my heart has burned within me at the glorious truths you have unfolded, and of which I have hitherto remained ignorant, while it has risen with indignation against the system of imposture by which the Church of Rome has so long held the great mass of mankind in subjection. From this moment, I come out of her; and may God give me grace to increase in knowledge of the truth, and to continue steadfast in it to the end!"

"Amen," said Mary and Humphrey.

From that day Reginald Clayton began to study the Scriptures, with the aid of his son, reading also the books he had collected. He rapidly improved in knowledge, his faith increased, and he soon became eager to instruct his neighbours and friends in the truths that had awakened him out of the sleep of death, and brought comfort and peace to his own soul.

Chapter 5

THE SPY

He who prayerfully reads the Word of God, seeking to find in it a guide to his feet, and comfort and food for his soul, will assuredly be amply rewarded. Mr. Clayton and his children found all, and more than they sought; and having found it, were eager to impart the glad tidings to their friends and neighbours, who, still ignorant of the truth as it is in Christ Jesus, remained bound by the fetters of the Church of Rome. Mr. Clayton, who had hitherto kept what religion he possessed to himself, now spoke out boldly to all he met of the value of the immortal soul—of the means by which its salvation can alone be secured.

But mark how he spoke. He said not a word against the Pope, or the Queen, or the authorities that existed—not even against the Church of Rome and her priests—but he spoke of the love of God for a perishing world. He spoke of that love which brought His Son Jesus down on earth to take on Him the form of man, of His sufferings, of His passion, of His sacrifice, whereby alone we obtain complete, perfect, and entire justification through faith and repentance. He spoke of His resurrection, and His glorious ascension into heaven, where He now sits at the right hand of God, our loving advocate with the Father, who, knowing our infirmities, in that He was tempted like us, can plead for us, pointing to His all-cleansing blood shed on Calvary.

Some of his hearers listened astonished to doctrines so strange to them. "What! Does Jesus Christ hear prayers without the intervention of the blessed Virgin, His mother, or of the saints?" they asked.

"Ay, Does He; for He says: 'Come unto me, all ye that labour and are heavy laden, and I will give you rest,'" answered Mr. Clayton. "I say nothing against the blessed Virgin, nor against the saints; but when I pray, I follow St. Paul's advice, and go direct to the throne of grace, where we have an advocate with the Father, Jesus Christ the righteous."

"But, surely, neighbour Clayton, we cannot gain heaven without penance and good works, and the prayers and offerings of the faithful to take us out of purgatory?"

"I say nothing about penance and good works," he answered, "but I do say that to be meet for heaven—to dwell for ever in the presence of the all-pure and holy God—we must have entire repentance of past sins, and faith in the atoning blood of His Son, which alone can wash away sin."

"Have you found all that in the Bible, Master Clayton?" asked another.

"Ay, much more than that, too," he answered. "If men lived according to the rules of the Bible, things would be very different to what they are at present; and this would be a very happy world instead of a most miserable one."

"But what say you, neighbours, to this burning of heretics, and such like doings? Surely that is according to the will of God; or His deputy on earth, our father the Pope, would not sanction them?" observed one, who evidently wished to entrap Mr. Clayton.

"If you can put another meaning on Christ's words, in His holy Gospel, (Matthew 5:44) 'But I say unto you, Love your enemies, bless them that curse you, do good to them that hate you, and pray for them which despitefully use you, and persecute you;' then, maybe, He who is all love and compassion wishes the Queen and her ministers thus to treat those so who differ with them in opinion."

Although Mr. Clayton was thus cautious in the way he put forth the truth as it is in Christ Jesus, yet it was impossible that he should escape giving offence to the authorities and priests of Rome should his words be repeated.

Humphrey and his sister were as eager as their father to speak to their young acquaintances of the glorious things they found in the Bible, and of their wonder that its study should be prohibited, while they endeavored to imitate his caution in the way they spoke of the existing system and authorities.

For some months they had thus gone on, attending diligently as before to their worldly affairs, but never neglecting to speak a word in season as opportunity offered. Thus the truth was making steady and quiet progress in this neighbourhood, in spite of the fires of Smithfield and the ragings of Bonner and his unquestioning followers.

Such was the state of things when a stranger appeared in the village seeking for lodgings. He was a decent sort of man, who had come out of London for the sake of quiet and country air. He took up his abode with a widow-woman, Mistress Darling by name, and paid liberally for all he required. He soon got into conversation with Mistress Darling on religious matters; and, though he did not speak decidedly in favour of the Reformed doctrines, his opinions seemed very moderate. He, however, soon wormed out of her, as far as she knew, what was said by her neighbours.

Soon after this, he contrived to meet Mr. Clayton, and to fall into conversation with him. He first talked on ordinary matters, and then let it appear that, though he had seldom seen the Bible, or read much of it, he was a humble inquirer after truth.

Cautious as before, Mr. Clayton, though acknowledging that he had read it, spoke only of the glorious doctrine it contains, avoiding even a word against those in authority who opposed its circulation. Day after day the stranger came and talked, and invariably turned the conversation on the important subject of religion. Nothing could be more calm and impartial than the way in which he spoke of the doctrines of the Reformation. At length, Mr. Clayton spoke out more freely than he had hitherto done; and Humphrey, with his usual warmth, hoping that the stranger might be converted to the truth, pressed home the Gospel on him, declaring his own conviction that, through it, and it alone, sinful man can be saved.

The stranger seemed well pleased to hear the youth speak thus, and, mildly turning to Mary, inquired whether she too held the same opinion as her father and brother. Mary frankly confessed that she did, and would die far rather than give up her treasure, now that she had once found it.

"But sooth, fair maiden, those opinions are such as have brought many to the faggot and stake; it might be wiser to deny them. Think of my words," he added, in a low tone of voice, looking intently at her.

Mary shuddered. There was an expression in those eyes she did not like.

Soon after, he bade them farewell, and his manner was as frank and cordial as before.

The next day, at the hour the stranger usually called, instead of him, Mistress Darling was seen hurrying up to the house, with grief and terror in her countenance.

"I pray thee, Mr. Clayton, get away from this; fly, fly; this is no safe place for you," she exclaimed, as soon as she got inside the house, and had recovered her breath, "neither for you, nor for your son nor daughter."

Astonished, Mr. Clayton inquired what she meant.

"I'll tell thee, and thou judge whether I am right in my suspicions," she replied. "I am not an eavesdropper nor a busybody, but still I am mistress in my own house, and have a right to know what goes on in it. I liked not altogether the ways of this Master Dixon, as he called himself, as he glided in and out, and spoke so smooth and oily like—inquiring about everybody, and what they thought and said. Now, I know well what your thoughts are, Master Clayton, about the Bible, and the right all who wish have to read it, and that you of times boldly speak out what you think. Then I saw Master Dixon often going to your house; and, thinks I to myself, if he is a true man, all well and good; but, if not, there's mischief in the wind."

"I hope, Mistress Darling that your fears are groundless," said Mr. Clayton. "Master Dixon seemed a straightforward, plain-spoken man; a master clothier, I understood, from London."

"Plainspoken, indeed, a more double-faced knave is not to be found within the borders of Essex," exclaimed Mistress Darling. "You shall hear and judge: Last night, when all decent folk should have been in bed, though I had been sitting up to do some necessary household work, I saw a bright light streaming from the door of my guest's chamber. Where the light came out, I could look in; and putting my eye to the chink, there I saw Master Dixon, the clothier as he called himself, leaning over a chest full of glittering vestments. He was taking off a crucifix and beads from his neck; and, as I am a true woman, instead of hair, which covered his head in the day, there was the shaven crown of the monk. I had seen enough to tell me what he is; and, fearful of being discovered, I hurried to bed.

"The next morning I tried to look as unconcerned as possible, but it was a hard matter, with his keen eyes piercing me through and through. Still he talked on as frankly as before; and, after he had broken his fast, he went forth; and when he came back, right glad was I to hear him say that he had ordered the Waggoner to call for his chest, and that he was minded to go a-foot that forenoon to London. On this, I edged in a word as best I could, about the love of all the people in these parts for Her Majesty the Queen, and all in authority under her; that I should just like to see the blessed Pope, and kiss his holy toe; and how all the people about here held to the ancient faith restored by Her Majesty the Queen, but he cut me short, asking me whether I thought that he had lost his wits and his hearing and sight; and as soon as he was out of the house, and clear through the village, I hurried off to warn you of the danger you are in."

"Thanks—thanks, Mistress Darling, for your warning; though I love not dissemblers, I feel sure that you thought to do no harm in thus speaking. For myself, I must take time to consider how to act."

Chapter 6

OPEN IN THE QUEEN'S NAME!

As soon as good Mistress Darling had left the house, Mr. Clayton called his son and daughter to him, and told them of what he had heard from her, and his belief that her suspicions were correct; and that their late visitor had drawn out their opinions for the purpose of betraying them.

"For myself, I wish to remain in my house and to follow in the course I have begun," he said; "if evil men desire to take my life, in God's hands I place it, and gladly will I yield it up at His summons; but with you, dear children, the case is different. You are not bound to continue here; you have years before you in which you may render Him faithful service."

Humphrey and Mary pleaded hard to be allowed to remain to support their father and to share his lot. Humphrey argued that Mistress Darling might have been mistaken, that it was cowardly to fly from a real danger, much more from a fancied one. Also, that to run away would appear as if they lacked confidence in God's power to protect them, and would dishonour Him among their neighbours.

Mr. Clayton, though against his judgment, at length consented to let his children remain with him. They had two old servants who had been with him, and his parents before him, from their childhood—John Goodenough and Susan Hobby. They were both called in, and the circumstances just become known were clearly explained to them.

"Whatever you please we should do, master, we will do," said John and Susan, repeating his words; "If you think fit to leave house and lands, and fly from the bloody-minded people who would prevent us from reading God's Word, then we will stay and watch over your interests, and guard the young master and Mistress Mary from harm, as far as in our power lies; but if they too must fly, then will our charge be less, but our sorrow and anxiety greater."

Mr. Clayton thanked his servants for their affections, but told them that he had resolved to remain at home, and trust to God's loving mercy and protection. If it were necessary that he should suffer as a witness of the truth, and for the confirming of the faith of many, he was ready to do so, assured that a crown of glory would be his, and that the cause of the Gospel would triumph in the end.

"If you can, however, persuade my dear children to go from home for a time, I shall be truly thankful," he added; "their lost mother's brother, William Fuller, resides at Berston, on the borders of the Salisbury Plain. It is a quiet spot, where Bishop Bonner will hardly think of sending his bloodhounds, or even such treacherous knaves as this Master Dixon, our late visitor. There they can remain till we see what happens. If I am let alone, they can return, and our happiness will be greater after the separation; but, if the fowlers come, they will find the young birds flown, to sing elsewhere God's praise, on some happier day; and only the old bird in the nest, who will prove but a tough morsel if they try to munch him."

"You hear, Master Humphrey, what your honoured father says," observed John Goodenough; "truly there is wisdom in his advice; small comfort would it give him, if he were taken to have you and sweet Mistress Mary snared also. Follow your honoured father's wishes in this matter, as you do in all others. No harm can come from your journey, and, may be, Mistress Darling has given us a false alarm, and all will go well. Though, truly, Master Dixon's eyes pleased me not," he muttered to himself; "no more shameless knave ever bore false witness against an honest man."

"May be," said Humphrey, "Master Dixon has sinister intentions regarding us, or may be not; but, on one point I am determined, unless my father commands me to leave him, come weal or woe, I'll stay and share his lot," exclaimed Humphrey stoutly.

"And so will I," said Mary, affectionately taking her father's hand. "You'll not send me from you, father?"

"Well! Well!" muttered John Goodenough, looking at them with a kind glance, and sighing, "It's the right thing, I doubt not; I should have done the same myself; but I would that I could not have got the dear young lady out of danger."

Notwithstanding the strong suspicions entertained against Master Dixon, Mr. Clayton hoped, however, that the alarm might prove false, and that he and his children might remain unmolested. One thing he determined, that as he had begun, so he would go on studying the Scriptures and enlightening the minds of his neighbours, as far as he had the power, with regard to the precious truths they contain. This he did, attending at the same time—steadily aided by Humphrey and Mary—to the affairs of his farm.

Their spirits rose, and their anxiety decreased, as day after day passed, and they remained unmolested. Two or three of Mr. Clayton's neighbours had begged to be allowed to come to his house on an evening, when the day's work was over, to hear him read and expound the Scriptures. Then another and another eager inquirer came, till their numbers increased to a dozen or more. With earnest prayer for enlightenment and simplicity of mind, not seeking for hidden meanings, or endeavoring to wrest Scripture to suit their own fancies, they showed forth the truth. Those meetings brought peace and joy and satisfaction to the hearts of all assembled. This, too, was almost in sight of the smoke ascending weekly from the fires in Smithfield, lit by the men who boasted that they were trampling out the Reformation in England.

It was the same throughout numberless towns and villages and hamlets in England. The priests of Rome were loudly boasting in the streets of their triumph. The Bible was being read at numberless firesides throughout the length and breadth of the land. To be sure, it was not read openly as now. Doors and windows, as in Mr. Clayton's house, were closely shut and barred; and, in some cases, persons were set to watch outside.

In that quiet village, where all were friendly and true, Mr. Clayton thought that simply to close and bar the windows and doors was all the precaution necessary.

One evening, he, with his family and several friends, were assembled in the old oak hall, where the whole household was wont to dine together. A hymn had been sung, prayers offered up, a portion of Scripture had been read, and Mr. Clayton was about to comment on it, when a loud knocking was heard, a voice exclaiming in a gruff tone— "Open! Open in the Queen's name, or we will batter in your door!" The members of the little congregation started to their feet; some who wore swords drew them mechanically; others grasped their staves, or seized on the stools on which they had sat.

Mr. Clayton stood up among them—no fear or agitation on his countenance— "Be calm, good neighbours," he said. "Put up your arms; no carnal weapons will avail us. This summons is for me, and me alone, I hope. I will open the door to these men; if they truly come with the Queen's authority, to that must I yield." The temper of those outside would not brook the delay which even these few words demanded; and even before Mr. Clayton could reach the door, it came crashing in—the open space it left being filled with armed men, who rushed forward, with swords and halberds (a combination spear and battle ax) uplifted, ready to cut down any who might oppose them. Resistance would have been useless, for already the hall was filled with the savage soldiers, and more appeared behind.

"Yield thee, Reginald Clayton," cried out their leader. "It is thee, and thy children we want alone at present—thy son and thy daughter—all of you accused of being determined and disobedient heretics. For the rest of you, my good folk, I will take your names, and come and fetch you when you are wanted."

"Though conscious of no crime, I yield to the authority of our liege lady, the Queen. Do with me what you list," said Mr. Clayton, with calm dignity; "but I crave indulgence for my young daughter, and beg that she may not be dragged from her home at night, and borne away to prison."

"My orders allow no alteration," answered the officer, in a somewhat softened tone, as he glanced at Mary, who stood pale and trembling near her brother, and endeavoring to avoid the bold gaze of the rough soldiers surrounding her. "I am to take you and your children forthwith to Newgate, there to await your trial on the charges brought against you. One favour I may take upon myself to grant. You have horses; let your servants saddle them; you may ride instead of going on foot, as you would otherwise have been compelled to do; for I had no orders to supply you with steeds."

Mr. Clayton and his children drew together, looking sadly in each other's countenances. Anger flashed from Humphrey's eye. "They dare not, they shall not hurt thee, dear sister," he whispered from his compressed lips; "they shall kill me first!"

"Dear children, we are in a state from which God can alone, if it His good will, deliver us," said Mr. Clayton solemnly. "I know not how long we may be together. Receive, then, the injunctions I lay on you. Hold to the truths you have learned from the Gospel. From that let nothing draw you; but if you have the opportunity, escape from the hands of these evil men. The time will come, and shortly, when the cause of the Gospel will be triumphant; and it would not be acting a wise part to throw away the chance of life, which may be employed in happier times in doing God's service."

"Father, I understand your wishes, and will obey them; though I would rather die with you than desert you," said Humphrey.

47

While they were speaking, the officer was taking down the names and callings of all present.

"Unless the priest gives a good report of you, varlets (scoundrels), remember that my next visit will be to carry you to be questioned by the Lord Bishop of London; and he is not over tender to those he finds to be heretics." No one answered; but many a prayer was offered up that all present might hold steadfast to the truth.

Finding that the orders of the officer were unchangeable, and that they must set forth that very night, Mr. Clayton ordered John Goodenough to get ready his horse, and another for Humphrey, with a pillion (large riding cushion) behind the saddle for Mistress Mary.

With a sad heart, John Goodenough went to obey. He came back, however, to Humphrey, for the key of the stable; and as he took it, he whispered— "Black Bess is a fleet steed and the night's dark; few know the country better than you; with fresh horses and other garments, I will be waiting at Ponder's Heath. No more at present."

John saw that the eyes of some of the soldiers were watching him; and, raising his voice, he added, "Keep her up well, Master, she's a sorry jade, but the only one fit to carry a pillion."

Humphrey was uncertain whether or not he should contemplate following John's suggestion. He looked at his sister; for her sake he would make the attempt to save her from the sufferings and foul contamination of a prison. Then he glanced at his father. Could he desert him in his great need?

Mr. Clayton seemed to know what John had said, and to divine his son's thoughts. Bending forward his head, he whispered, "There is One who will never forsake me; for He has said it. Do as John advises."

The officer having taken down the names, residences, and occupations of all the persons present, called loudly for food for himself and his men.

Mr. Clayton replied that it should be forthwith placed before them, and desired Susan to prepare such provisions as the house could furnish.

She moved about, however, without any of her usual enthusiasm; and, when the officer began to complain of her tardiness, declared that she had been so upset by the alarm to which she had been exposed, that she could not remember where the things were placed, and must wait until John's return, that he might assist her.

John, also, had never before taken so much time to saddle a couple of horses; and, at length, the officer ordered two of his men to go and hasten the servant. No sooner, however, did they put their heads out of doors, than they came back, saying that the rain was coming down in torrents; and asked whether they should go and bring him.

"No; stay, knaves!" answered the officer, "and as that servant does not come, go help the woman find the provender, or find it for yourselves; and some strong ale or sack, if that is forthcoming."

Susan, by degrees, seemed to recover her wits; and, making up the fire, with the aid of her military assistants, a hot supper was placed on the table round which the readers of the Scriptures had lately been assembled. One by one, most of the former guests went out, taking a sorrowful farewell of their host, knowing too well that it might be the last time they should ever see him. The officer now invited him, and Humphrey, and Mary to come and partake of the good cheer that had been prepared. Humphrey was about indignantly to refuse, but a look from his father made him curb his anger and accept the invitation. To Mary, also, Mr. Clayton remarked, "You have a long ride before you, dear girl, you will require sustenance; take it now, while you can."

"Yes, in truth, father," said Humphrey, assuming a tone of cheerfulness he little felt, "it is wise to lay a store in our insides, and to fill our wallets to boot; for I conclude,

Master Officer, that the gentry in Newgate do not get over-daintily or over plentifully fed?"

"No, by my troth. Black bread and water is their daily fare; and that none the best," answered the officer. "But you are a wise lad; and you shall have no hindrance from taking as much as you can carry. Put up, too, a bottle of this good sack; I'll help you to drain it before the night is over.

"You have before you the only three bottles we had in the house, or I would thankfully obey you," answered Humphrey. "We do not often indulge in wine in the country."

"I doubt it not, lad; strong ale is more suited to the palates of you farmers; in truth, I doubt not you'll live to drink many a flagon if, when you are brought before the Bishop of London, you stick not too firmly to your opinions, and just say an Ave Maria, and a Paternoster or so, to show that you are a good son of mother Church, and no heretic."

"May God strengthen me to hold to the truth," said Humphrey, in a low tone, lifting his eyes to Heaven.

"Well, well; you'll think my advice good when you come before Bishop Bonner, and he brings his arguments before you," observed the officer, with a significant look, which made poor Mary shudder.

Supper over, he became impatient to depart; but John Goodenough had not come with the horses, nor indeed had the rain ceased. At length John bustled in, his dress showing the state of the weather. "It's beastly dirty work catching a horse in a night like this; and I never thought that the old mare would give me so much trouble," he exclaimed.

Goodenough busied himself with helping Mary to mount, while a farm-servant held their master's horse. Mr. Clayton would have been more than human had he not felt cast down as he took a farewell of his home, which he knew he might probably never see again.

Chapter 7

THE RIDE IN THE NIGHT

Dark and dreary was the night when Reginald Clayton and his son and daughter set forth on their journey to London. They had a ride of sixteen miles or more before they could reach Newgate, where the officer declared that they must be lodged by midnight. The wind had lulled and the rain had ceased as they passed through the door of their beloved home to mount their horses.

Mr. Clayton spoke only a few words to his son. "Remember my wishes," he said, as he rode on with the officer and the other men who had him in charge.

"Hold up Black Bess, Master Humphrey, and she'll carry you and the young mistress safely," said John Goodenough, as he helped Mary on her pillion, and wrapped her hood closely round her. "No fear of her running away on you."

"You'll not ride too fast, I hope, gentlemen, for the good old jade is not so strong on her legs as she used to be, and little accustomed to midnight travelling," added John, addressing the soldiers.

"No fear of that," answered one of the soldiers, "our beasts have had a hard day's work already, and it would not be easy to get them out of a walk."

"So much the better; you hear that, Mistress Mary; so you need not be afraid," said John.

"Forward!" cried the officer, and the cavalcade moved on. A fierce blast swept along the road at that instant, followed by vivid lightning, with a rattling peal of thunder, which made even the troopers' tired steeds spring from side to side. Humphrey had the greatest difficulty in making Black

Bess maintain the character John Goodenough had given her, for in truth she was noted for her strength and speed, and spirit also, though so docile that Mary could ride her herself. Had not the men been engaged in tranquilizing their own horses, they would have perceived the difficulty their young prisoner had to keep his steed quiet. Mr. Clayton's horse, also a fine animal, sprang forward; and his rider might easily have made his escape, had he thought fit to attempt it.

"If you keep not close to me, I must fire. My life is answerable for your safe custody. Close up there—close up from the rear!" shouted the officer.

The order was obeyed, and the party moved on. This blast was the restart of the storm. The lightning flashed, and the thunder roared, and the rain came down in torrents, the darkness being so intense that the horsemen could scarcely see their way. The officer would gladly have again sought the shelter of Mr. Clayton's house; but he remembered that his orders did not give him the option of remaining in the event of bad weather, and he pushed on. The road, as they approached the then small town of Romford, was low and level, and the horses floundered with increasing difficulty. Faithful John Goodenough had so carefully wrapped up Mary in a thick woolen cloak and hood, that she had hitherto, in spite of the rain remained dry; but now, as she looked out from under the covering, and could see nothing beyond the dark expanse of rushing water which surrounded her, she trembled with fear for her father's and brother's and her own safety.

"Hold fast on, dear sister, and do not be alarmed; I know the road, and Black Bess knows it too; and we shall soon be on dry ground again," said Humphrey, as he slowly walked his horse through the flood in company with three or four of the troopers, who could not make their tired steeds keep up with those of their companions. They were indeed floundering on in a way that made it very doubtful whether they would be in a condition to overtake the rest of the party, who were lost to sight in the darkness ahead, and whose voices, as they shouted to each other to keep up, grew fainter and fainter.

Humphrey kept steadily on; and as he observed the number of his guard decreasing, he began seriously to contemplate the possibility of escaping. He wished to do so—not for his own sake, for nothing would have induced him to leave his father; but for the sake of preserving his beloved sister from the insults and cruel treatment to which she would too probably be exposed. He did not consult her in the matter. If he could save her, he would. She most likely would have felt as he did, and would have been willing to undergo death itself, rather than desert her father.

He had not misunderstood their father's words, nor John Goodenough's hints. If an opportunity offered, he was bound to take advantage of it. A little out of Romford, he knew that a road turned off to the right; and the banks were higher there than in other places, and crowned with thick trees, so that the darkness would likewise be greater. At length, the horsemen floundered out of the flood, and a few scattered lights from the houses at Romford, shining dimly through the rain, appeared before them.

Much to Humphrey's disappointment, they here found the rest of the party waiting for them. The officer soundly rated the men for not keeping up with him; but they declared that they had done their best; and that even the prisoners' old horse, carrying two persons, had got through the flood better than theirs. He, undoubtedly, would gladly have taken shelter in the town, but that he was compelled by his orders to push on, and that no doors were open to receive him and his company. So, with many a wistful glance at the windows, and thoughts of the good cheer perhaps to be found within, the soldiers rode out of the town once more into the country.

They were approaching the turning which Humphrey remembered leading towards Hertfordshire. The four men who had especial charge of him rode on either side, as before.

Now was the best opportunity he could hope for of escaping. Should he let it pass? Yet how could he hope to pass the two horsemen on his right side, without being stopped? Alone he could easily do it, but might there be some chance for his sister to receive some injury in the attempt?

While he was considering, the matter was settled for him; for suddenly there was a loud crash, as if a tree had fallen across the road; there was the sound of scuffling of feet; the two guards on his right were jerked from their saddles to the ground; he felt his own rein seized, and his horse led to the right, while the other two guards, with oaths, exclaimed that their reins had been cut through. Not a word had hitherto been spoken by the assailants, but a voice which sounded strangely like that of John Goodenough, exclaimed, "Ride on, Master Humphrey; ride on, and we'll follow."

He took the advice, and Black Bess dashed onwards along the road to the right. He could hear the troopers shouting and swearing, some at not being able to catch their horses, and others at being unable to guide them; while those in advance, having turned to ascertain what was the matter, had tumbled over the branches or other impediments thrown across the road.

He had not gone far, however, when he heard the loud clattering of hoofs in pursuit of him. Black Bess, though, bore him and his sister right gallantly; and he felt sure that, if he could keep ahead of his pursuers for some time, he should be able to distance them completely.

Still his pursuers were getting terribly near; great, therefore, was his satisfaction when he heard John Goodenough's voice shout out: "Pull in the rein, Master Humphrey; the knaves will be in no condition to follow for some minutes, and we've a long ride before us, if Mistress Mary is able to take it."

"Oh, yes, yes; whatever you wish," said Mary.

"But my father! Oh, he may suffer for this, if he has not also escaped."

"He forbade me attempting his rescue; and if I had, it would likely enough have miscarried. He will not be made to suffer more because you have escaped; and his heart will be far, far lighter," answered John. "But I do not say that we are not to push on; though I have little fear that our steeds will keep well ahead of the troopers, even if the whole of them were to come after us."

To Humphrey's inquiries as to how his rescue had been arranged, John told him that he had resolved on it directly the officer had said that he should take the prisoners to London that night—that he had immediately gone to several of his friends, who had agreed to ride on, and attempt a rescue at the spot he had chosen; and that he had followed, by cross cuts, as soon as they had left the house.

The brother and sister were thankful at their unexpected escape. Still they had many dangers to go through and risks of being recaptured.

John told them, however, that he had prepared disguises for them; and that it was important that they should get to the other side of London before daylight.

Chapter 8

AN EXCITING JOURNEY

God orders all things for the best for those who trust in Him; yet how little can we tell what is the best for us. The fearful storm, which raged, seemed to increase the sufferings of those who had been thus cruelly torn from their home; yet it greatly assisted the escape of Humphrey and his sister. Had the night been fine, they would have encountered many wayfarers, and questions as to where they were going would have been asked; but the rain kept every one within, and they passed through even thickly populated villages without being seen. John's spirits, too, rose, as the chance of being over-taken decreased; and he laughed as he described the way in which he and two other men had so completely discomforted a party of the Queen's soldiers.

"They'll never suppose that two or three Brentwood men did the work, and still less confess it; but they'll affirm that they were set on by an ambush of fifty or a hundred outlaws from Epping, and that in the confusion you managed to make your escape."

His thoughts, however, very soon went back to his master. Still he was inclined to look on the bright side of things, and he endeavored to persuade Humphrey and Mary of what he was himself inclined to believe, that Mr. Clayton might yet escape without compromising his principles. Humphrey could not himself entertain such hopes; but, as his great wish was to keep up his sister's spirits till he could place her in safety, he made no reply on the subject.

As the dawn broke the rain ceased, and just as the sun rose they found themselves in front of a cottage, on the borders of a wide heath, with a thick wood extending away on one side.

"It is a good thing to have relations and friends scattered about the world, to whom one may apply in a difficulty; my sister's husband's brother lives there, Thomas Holden by name, an honest man, who long since embraced the truths of the Gospel; but happily for himself, living a quiet, almost solitary life, has escaped persecution. He will, I know, gladly receive and conceal you, and aid you in proceeding on your way. My duty is to return home, to look after the farm."

Humphrey was unwilling to risk the safety of the good man by taking shelter in his cottage, but John overruled all his objections, and assured him that it would afford the greatest satisfaction to Thomas Holden to assist a fellow-worshipper.

John knocked at the door of the cottage. Scarcely had he done so, when it was opened by a sturdy, open-faced man, with a florid complexion and light hair, whose countenance beamed with pleasure as he saw him. As briefly as possible, while the party were dismounting, John explained their errand.

"Help them! that I will, friends, God willing. A bed shall be ready for the young mistress, and dry clothes and mug of good warm ale for the master, and we will bestow the steeds where no popish knaves will easily find them. My good wife is just a-foot. Here, Cicely! Cicely, come forth and see to our friends!" A comely-looking dame on hearing this made her appearance, and took the poor, weary girl under her motherly care. Thomas having attended to the most urgent wants of his guests, hurried off with their tired steeds towards the wood, where, he said, in a shed he had there erected, he hoped that they might remain concealed till ready again to proceed on their journey.

John accompanied Thomas Holden that he might find the horses, if required.

Left to himself, Humphrey had time to reflect on his sister in safety; and probably she would be exposed to less danger by remaining where she was, with the honest woodman, than in performing the long journey into Wiltshire; still, his father had wished him, in case of danger, to take refuge in his relation's house, and he therefore finally resolved to proceed.

John Goodenough had brought disguises. His was that of a woodcutter of the poorest class; his sister's that of a peasant girl. He had taken his from the bundle, which had gotten damp, and dried them, and put them on by the time the men returned.

Mrs. Holden suggested that, by the application of a mixture containing walnut-juice and other ingredients, which she knew how to prepare, his appearance would be still more completely altered. In the same manner Mary was so completely disguised that when she entered the sitting room, Humphrey scarcely knew her.

John looked at them approvingly. "Little fear now, me-thinks, but what you may both travel through England, and none of Bishop Bonner's blood-hounds will recognize you," he observed.

It was important, however, that they all should take some rest, for the night had been to them one of great mental and bodily fatigue.

John, however, though grieving to part from his young master and mistress, was anxious to be at home to attend to the necessary duties of the farm, which Susan could ill perform alone. He knew, also, that if discovered to be absent, it would be suspected that he had taken part in the rescue of his young master and mistress. For the same reason it would be dangerous to take Black Bess back, and she must, therefore, remain concealed in Holden's wood hut. After John had, therefore, taken a brief rest and some more food, he bade Humphrey and Mary farewell, hoping to reach home soon after daybreak.

Mary likewise declared herself capable of resuming the journey at once, and Thomas Holden insisted on accompanying them part of the way. He had a friend who lived some twelve miles off, and it was arranged that they should try and reach his cottage on Black Bess, who might be concealed in the neighbourhood, while, afterwards, Mary could ride a donkey or a pony, and Humphrey could go afoot, a fitting way for him to proceed according to the character he had assumed.

The greater portion of the rest of the day was spent in taking that rest the young travellers so greatly needed, except for a short time when Humphrey repeated to Thomas Holden and his wife certain portions of Scripture of the many he had committed to memory, for, alas! they had no Bible to read.

As soon as it grew dark, Thomas brought Black Bess to the door, with another rough, but strong steed, which he was accustomed to ride. His good wife did not forget provisions, and put up enough to last them for several days. The weather had become fine and mild, and as Black Bess seemed in no way tired, they hoped to reach their destination at the time Holden calculated they might do so.

Mary bore up wonderfully well, notwithstanding the fatigue she had to endure, for the road was bad, and they were compelled to proceed at a rapid rate. Those were not times when people ventured abroad at night, unless under pressing necessity, and they therefore met no one to question them.

At dawn, they reached the house of an honest yeoman, Richard Ellis, long known to Thomas Holden as a sincere, Christian man. He proved it by receiving the young travellers without questioning; and when he heard of the difficulties they were in, promised to befriend them to the best of his power. He was of a superior station to Holden, and possessed of more wealth and more education also. He possessed a Bible, which, in spite of the proclamations and threats of Queen Mary and her Government, he persisted in reading to his family as well as to himself. He pressed Humphrey and

Mary to remain a whole day and night to rest before continuing their journey.

As soon as it was dusk, the windows were closed, lights brought in, and the family assembled. He then prayed with them, and read the Scriptures, and expounded what he had read. It was a blessed thing to have that book, and Humphrey and his sister spent their time during their stay in reading it. They found it truly a great comfort and consolation in their trouble, as all will who seek it in the spirit they did. Thus strengthened in mind and body, they set forth under the new characters they had assumed.

They purposed saying, if questioned, that they had been deprived of their father and mother, and that they were going to a relative in the South of England who could afford them employment and support.

Richard Ellis gave them his blessing and his prayers as they quitted his house at early dawn, before any one was afoot to observe them. Richard Ellis had provided for Mary a small, rough pony, but very docile and sure-footed. After proceeding for about two hours, they stopped to break their fast, and rest on a green bank by the side of a rippling stream, beneath the shade of a wide-spreading oak, while their pony fed quietly near them without attempting to stray. Here, too, they were able to offer up their prayers for their father's safety, and for guidance and protection for themselves.

Then again they journeyed on, avoiding the hostels where they would meet strangers, who might ask questions not easily answered. They resolved, therefore, to rest instead in barns or sheds, or even under some thick-leaved tree with cloaks and a coverlid, with which Humphrey was able to wrap her up so completely at night that she was protected from the chill air of night. The weather remained fine; and so well pleased was Mary with this, to her, a new style of couch, under the canopy of heaven that she begged that the practice might be continued to the end of the journey.

One of the risks they ran was being stopped as vagrants—houseless wanderers—against whom severe acts then existed; their mean dresses and apparent poverty would save them from the danger of being robbed, they hoped. Thus, day after day, they journeyed on, seldom making good more than twenty miles in the right direction, for the roads were rough and the paths they took often circuitous.

They had discarded all fear of being traced, although that was in reality the greatest danger they ran. Still, had they been aware of it, they could not have followed any other course than to travel straight on, and pray to God for protection.

At length, late one evening, the borders of Salisbury Plain were reached; Berston was on the other side of it. In a thick wood, near at hand, they hoped to find shelter for the night; nor were they disappointed. A woodcutter had been at work there, and had left a pile of faggots ready to be carried away.

With these Humphrey was able to build a hut for his sister, affording abundance of shelter. There was plenty of grass, too, for their pony; and a stream running by not far off, gave them a supply of water. Thankful for the safety they had hitherto enjoyed, they looked forward to crossing the plain on the morrow. Having offered up their prayer of thanksgiving, they laid themselves down to rest under their leafy shelter.

Humphrey awoke just as the first streaks of dawn could be seen through the trunks of the tall trees. He aroused his sister. "It will be well to get to our uncle's house before anything may take him abroad," he observed. "It will be better, too, to leave this wood before we are seen; for we cannot err on the side of caution." Accordingly, after they had said their prayers, without waiting to break their fast, Humphrey called the pony, which now came at his voice, lured by a piece of bread. Mary mounted it, while the shades of night still lingered in the west.

In those days, when sign-posts, mile-stones, and other means by which travellers might direct their course did not exist, the faculties of people were more sharpened than at presently is often the case. Humphrey had discreetly inquired the direction of Berston. He was thus able, by carefully noticing the spot where the sun rose, to guide his course with tolerable accuracy towards it. Had the day been misty, or overcast with clouds, his difficulty would have been considerable. They had proceeded some way, when, in the distance, rose what seemed a row of huge stones, standing upright, with others placed on their tops.

"Those must form the temple of Stonehenge, built by our ignorant ancestors, when the religion of the Druids was that of the land," remarked Humphrey, as he pointed them out to his sister.

"Yet, methinks, dark and cruel as was their faith, it is scarcely more cruel or senseless than that which Queen Mary and her Spanish husband, King Philip, wish to establish again in poor England. The Druids offered up human sacrifices to their gods, because they believed them to be cruel and bloodthirsty. These people burn and torture their fellow-creatures in the name of a pure, gentle, and loving Saviour, because they read the book He has sent them, and wish to worship Him in the way that Book points out—in spirit and truth."

"Oh, dear sister, we have cause to be thankful that we have been brought out from among them, even though persecution and troubles have come on us. Whatever happens, let us hold fast to the truth."

While still travelling over the plain, they recognized a house in the far distance. They directed their course towards it; and Humphrey, going to the door, inquired of a somewhat slight, fair-haired man, with a kind expression of countenance, which was the residence of William Fuller?

"I am that person," was the answer, "but what, lad, can you require of me?"

"I am your nephew, Humphrey Clayton; and I come with my sister, by my father's desire, to crave your protection," answered Humphrey.

"You my nephew! He is a fair youth, and she, too, is fair, and would scarcely appear in such guise as yours," said Mr. Fuller, gazing incredulously at the young people.

Humphrey now told him what had occurred, and of the peril in which their father was placed.

"Protect thee! That I will, dear children," exclaimed William Fuller, a look of affectionate regard coming over his countenance, "Protect thee! I will, God willing, against Pope and Queen, and Bishop Bonner and his bloodhounds to boot, as long as I have the power. Ah! And any one persecuted for the faith, much more thee and thy sweet sister there. Come in, come in; and food and rest, and fresh clothing shall be provided for thee both."

A boy was called to take the pony round to a shed, and the young travelers were ushered into the house, where Mrs. Fuller soon made her appearance, and gave them as hearty a welcome as had her husband.

Chapter 9

A REFUGE INDEED

"I truly rejoice that you and your sister have sought me out by your father's desire," said Mr. Fuller, when the young people, having changed their garments, had joined him in the sitting room, where a substantial meal was prepared for them. "I loved your father for your dear mother's sake, as well as for his own; and grieved that he should remain with his mind darkened, and bound by the shackles of Rome. He knew that I, long ago, was freed from bondage, and also that your mother believed the truth as it is in Christ Jesus, and constantly prayed for his conversion; but, till you arrived to-day, I knew not that her prayers had been heard. It is wonderful news that he, and you two, her dear children, had been called into the marvelous light of the Gospel.

"As I think of it, my children, my heart bounds with joy and gratitude; and oh, dear children, how will her blessed spirit rejoice when she knows, as assuredly she will know in heaven above, that he whom she loved on earth is ready to confess his Saviour before men, and to go forth even unto death, as a witness of the truth.

"You shed tears for the danger in which your father is placed. They are natural tears, and such as God will not condemn; but think, dear children, at the same time, of the words of our blessed Lord, 'Also I say unto you, Whosoever shall confess me before men, him shall the Son of man also confess before the angels of God,' (Luke 12:8)."

"Yes, uncle; indeed, I know well the words of the blessed Gospel, and gladly, even now, would I return to London, that I might bear witness to the truth in company with my dear father," exclaimed Humphrey, with his usual warmth.

"My nephew, I do not advise you to pursue such a course," answered Mr. Fuller. "Your duty was to come to me as you have done. You may not be required to give your life for the truth; and God may have some other work for you to do, in which you can equally confess Him before men, and make known His name, and advance His honour and glory in the world."

These arguments somewhat reconciled Humphrey to the course he had pursued, though he did not the less desire to return to share his father's captivity and ultimate fate, whatever that might be. His uncle, however, did not allow him to think in silence.

"You must tell me, Humphrey," he continued, "how this happy conversion was brought about. I know there is but one agent, one teacher, one guide—the Holy Spirit, who can convert the heart of a man, and enlighten the mind; and yet wonderful and numerous are the means employed."

Humphrey narrated to his uncle and aunt the chief events that had occurred in their family from the day he and his sister had witnessed the martyrdom of William Hunter to the present time.

"Ah! Yes; our arch-enemy, Satan, believes when he instigates his wretched tools to shed the blood of the saints, that he is about to trample out the truth; instead of which, for every martyr who dies, hundreds, nay thousands, are rescued from the kingdom of darkness, and brought into the kingdom of heaven.

"When Satan instigated Judas to betray our blessed Lord, he undoubtedly thought that he had gained a victory. Still more did he rejoice when he saw Him hanging on the cross, not understanding that thus the Son of God had become the Saviour of the world, that the seed of the woman whose heel he had bruised had accomplished that glorious prophecy uttered to our first parents, and that he was to find that thus his head had been bruised. Who but Satan—who but Anti-christ—is the instigator of all the cruel burnings that are now taking place?

"And yet, cruel as are those who expect thus to trample out the truth, they are even yet more foolish, for they are pursuing the very and surest way to make Englishmen hate the very name of Rome and the Pope of Rome. It is securing the ultimate triumph of Protestant principles throughout the land. Be assured, dear children that the glorious Gospel will be heard throughout the length and breadth of England in spite of Philip of Spain and our unhappy Queen.

"These opinions I have held for many years, and though I grieve to hear of Christian men suffering imprisonment and death, yet my faith in the certainty of the progress of the Gospel is in no way shaken.

"I have long lived a quiet life in this retired place, and though I have never concealed my opinions, and lost no opportunity of imparting to my neighbours a knowledge of the truth, I have hitherto escaped persecution, yet have I ever been prepared for it. I foresaw that bad times were coming for England—a long night, although day, I felt sure, would break in the end—when Philip of Spain came over to wed the Queen.

"That year of 1554 I went up to London on business, and saw the preparations being made for the reception of the Queen's intended husband. When our blessed young King Edward the Sixth came to the throne, and showed his love for the Gospel, I had vainly supposed that Popery would, ere long, be totally abolished from the land. Albeit I considered that too much conformity with the Romish ritual was still maintained in the form of worship he had sanctioned, calculated to lead the people back to, rather than away from, the errors of the Papal system. Alas, what sights was I to behold! What grievous backslidings among all ranks of people!

"One of the saddest sights was to see hundreds, nay thousands, of married ministers turned out of their houses, with their wives and little ones literally begging their bread, or starving, as many did, and their places filled by the priests of Rome, who had restored all the ceremonial observances which had been swept away, who were singing masses for the souls of the departed, hearing confession, granting absolution, causing the adoration of the Eucharist, and teaching the fable of Transubstantiation; while the Holy Bible—which even the Queen's father, Henry, had allowed the people everywhere freely to possess and read—albeit he was little influenced by its sacred precepts, was now a prohibited book.

"One of those true ministers of the Gospel has since been residing with us, though in disguise, for fear of our enemies. I found him in the last stage of exhaustion, when he had already lost his beloved wife and two infant children. He is from the house at this present moment, but will return in the evening, and he will tell you of many things of which probably you know little. You cannot fail to be interested in what he will say, as well as in himself, for a more faithful, humble Christian does not breathe, so full of confidence in our Heavenly Father's mercy, so full of love for the souls of his fellow-creatures.

"However, to my history. As Mary was looked on by many Protestants, as well as by the Papists, as the rightful heir to the throne, she was heartily welcomed when she arrived in London to assume the sceptre, few persons dreaming of the blood which was so soon cruelly to be shed at her command. I cannot even now think without tears of the execution of that young, beautiful, and talented Christian woman, the Lady Jane Grey. It was a bad beginning, and Protestant men began to tremble for their religious liberty.

"A greater reason had they to fear when it became known that the Queen had resolved to marry Philip of Spain, one of the most bigoted princes of Europe. You have heard how many, dreading the consequences of having a foreigner and Papist as king, who would be eager to put England again under the power of the Pope, took up arms to prevent the marriage. I do not for one moment approve of an appeal to arms. God's work is not thus to be accomplished. It is a hard thing for unregenerate man to wait patiently for what God may think fit to bring about in His own way. In this instance the result proves strongly that I am right in my opinion.

"In Devonshire, Sir Thomas Carew, with a body of friends, took up arms to resist the landing of the King of Spain, but finding that he was not supported as he had expected, he fled for safety to France. In the meantime, in Kent, a confederate of Carew's, Sir Thomas Wyatt, also rose in arms, and soon, many of the Queen's troops going over to him, he advanced with a small and ill-disciplined army towards London.

"There was great terror and alarm in the city at the approach of this army, which came without difficulty to Charing Cross, opposite St. James's Palace. Here one part of Sir Thomas's force separated from him to attack Whithall; while he, with the rest, advanced on through Temple Bar and Fleet Street, till they came to Lud Gate, which they found closed against them. From this, after some skirmishing, they turned hack purposeless.

"There was another skirmish at Temple Bar, when Wyatt was persuaded to yield himself up a prisoner under the expectation of being pardoned. In this he was cruelly disappointed, and not only he, but also some score of his misguided followers paid the penalty of their rebellion with their lives. Oh! It was a sad sight to see their lifeless bodies hanging on gibbets (gallows) at the end of every street in London. Truly, it sickened the people of rebellion, but it did not make them love the Queen more.

"When however, news was received that King Philip was actually coming, the bodies were taken down, and the gibbets removed, and people prepared to put on smiling faces to welcome him. At length he arrived at Southampton, attended by a gorgeous train of Castilian and Flemish nobles, and the Queen went down to Winchester to welcome him. Gardiner, Bishop of Winchester, married them on the festival of St. James, the guardian saint of Spain.

"At first, even Philip and Gardiner, though acknowledging that they desired to see the nation brought back to the Church of Rome, talked only of mild means. They talked of trusting to persuasion and eloquence to convert the people. They were soon to throw off the mask, and to show what Rome is when opposed, and when she has the power in her hands. She was mild and gentle enough in Edward the Sixth's time, she is mild enough in the States of these German Princes who have thrown off her power; but, alas, now we know her as she is, and as she will ever be, under similar circumstances.

"Yes, Rome, in her arrogance and bigotry, hates the light, and believes, and ever will believe, that she can stamp it out with her iron-shod heel and her burning brands.

"After a few days of banqueting, Mary and Philip proceeded to Windsor, that the new king might be installed as a Knight of the Garter. It was then, as was supposed by the Queen's order, a herald took down the arms of England, and in their place would have put up those of Spain, but the indignation of some lords was so great that he was compelled to restore them.

"A few days after this the King and Queen returned to London. The public places were decorated to do them honour. On the conduits of Cracechurch were painted portraits of the nine worthies, and of Henry VIII, and Edward VI. Henry was painted; I remember it well, with a Bible in his hand, on which was written *Verbum Dei*. Bishop Bonner, having noted the book in the King's hand, shortly afterwards called the painter before him, and with vile words and other abuse, such as "traitor, knave," demanded who bade him describe the King with a book in his hand—threatening to send him to the Fleet. The painter humbly replied that he thought he had done no harm. How could he, for what more gracious and important act did the King ever perform than when he ordered that the Bible should be read in all churches throughout the realm? 'Nay,' replied the Bishop, 'it is against the Queen's catholic proceedings.' So, shortly afterwards, the painter put out the book of *Verbum Dei,* and placed instead in his hand a new pair of gloves. When I saw that change as I walked along the street, I knew well that bad times were coming for poor England—an empty pair of gloves for the full free Gospel of truth! Bad times have come.

"Popery has come back, and is rampant in the land; but still, the truth is here. They cannot take that away—they cannot put that out while a faithful man remains to keep the lamp alight. But we have talked long enough. You shall now return to your room and rest awhile till our evening meal is prepared."

Humphrey gladly obeyed, but he could not rest.

The window of the sleep-room, which had been awarded to him, opened over the plain. As he was looking out of it, he saw in the far distance a party of horsemen passing across it. He watched them anxiously. For what purpose could they have come? Could it be that they had traced him and his sister thus far? If so, he prayed that even at the last they might lose trace of them, for it would be doubly grievous to bring their uncle into trouble for having given them shelter. Now it seemed that the horsemen were approaching the house.

Humphrey felt that he ought to give his uncle notice, that he and Mary might be concealed in time; but just as he was leaving the window they again turned away, and continued their course across the heath.

The matter, when Humphrey mentioned it, caused some anxiety in the family, at the same time it showed that if Humphrey and his sister's pursuers had traced them in that direction, they could be guided by no certain information as to where they purposed seeking refuge.

William Fuller was a wise and cautious man, and at the same time stout of heart. He firmly resolved to prevent it being known that they were secreted in his house. Their pony was concealed during the day that it might be removed to a distance at night; and the boy alone who had seen them arrive, and one female servant were aware that they were in the house, both being earnestly cautioned not to speak on the matter.

Anxiety and fatigue had sorely tried Mary's health, and it was evident that many days would be required to restore it. Humphrey quickly regained his strength, and as soon as he saw Mary in a fair way of recovery, he told his uncle of his resolve to return to London, that he might comfort and aid his father as best he could, or be ready to suffer with him.

"I cannot gainsay thee, nephew. I, under like circumstances, would have done the same," answered William Fuller; "yet consider well what would be thy father's wish; that should guide thee."

Chapter 10

THE HERETIC
FACES THE BISHOP

We now return to Reginald Clayton. The rage of the officer was very great when he discovered that his younger prisoners had escaped, it being increased by fear, as he dreaded the penalties he would have to suffer when it was known that he had arrived without them, and that it was natural that they should have attempted to escape, seeing the treatment to which it was likely they would be exposed.

Calling a halt, the officer shouted to the troopers who had had charge of the younger prisoners to go in chase of them, but this order was more easily given than obeyed, seeing that two had lost their horses altogether, and that the other two had had their bridles cut through, and could in no ways mend them in the dark. They, however, replied that they would forthwith obey, and the rest of the cavalcade moved forward.

In those days prisons were truly places of punishment, foul, dark, and damp dungeons, into which those accused of crime, as well as those found guilty of the most heinous, were indiscriminately huddled together. Into such a place Reginald Clayton was thrown, and with him his son and fair young daughter would have been thrown likewise.

Many of those among whom he found himself were accused of heresy, and others of murder, highway robbery, house-breaking, cattle-stealing, thefts of all sorts, who would, if found guilty, have to answer for their crimes with their lives.

Yet these men of all others, took a strange delight in insulting and abusing him on account of his heresy, telling

73

him that he would assuredly burn, because he put no faith in the Pope or the Mass, and obeyed not the Queen or Bishop Bonner. When he could, Mr. Clayton avoided speaking, and when he was compelled to speak, he replied with mildness and dignity "that he acted only according to what he believed to be a right judgment, wishing to offend no man."

He had been in this abode of wretchedness and crime for about three days, when he heard his name called, and found at the gate of the cell the officer who had brought him there.

"Art thou ready to take another ride, Master Clayton, though not so far?" asked the officer. "The Lord Bishop of London has sent to talk to thee. If thou art a wise man, thou wilt answer him discreetly."

"To the best of my power, and in accordance with the truth, I will," answered Mr. Clayton, as he was conducted to the courtyard where a horse stood ready for him. There were sights in London in those days happily not to be seen at present. Friars and priests walking about in gaudy vestments, with censers swinging, and bells tinkling, and figures of the Virgin and Child, or of saints, held aloft; and gibbets at the end of most thoroughfares, some with men still hanging on them, rebels taken in arms; and others with the chains or ropes alone remaining, to which they had been attached; and then there were people dragged along, unwillingly, to be whipped, or imprisoned, or hung, or maybe, to be burnt.

Seldom did many weeks pass by, during the good Queen's reign, without people being taken to Smithfield, or into Essex, or elsewhere, to be executed, to remind the lieges of their blessings, and of the advantages to be gained by the complete restoration of the Roman Catholic faith in Old England.

As Reginald Clayton rode on, he took note of these things and, disregarding himself, he prayed that his country might be delivered from the bondage under which she groaned, and remain forever after truly Protestant.

At length he reached the palace of the Bishop, and was placed in an anteroom, where guards with drawn weapons were stationed. There were several other persons of various degrees waiting to be examined on their religious opinions. They were not prohibited from conversing with each other. Some had before been under examination, some were wavering, some firm, and some had been taken up for idle words spoken at random, without much knowledge of the truth.

"Verily this is a time, friends, above all others, when we should be able to give a reason for the hope that is within us," observed a grave and aged divine, who was within three days to seal his opinions with his blood.

Among them all there was, however, but little fear or trembling. At length Reginald Clayton was called in. The Bishop was seated at a heavy oak table, in a huge armchair. His cap was somewhat thrown back, a frown was on his brow, a sneer on his lips. A keen-eyed priest, with shaven crown, who acted as his secretary, sat at the end of the table taking notes. Bonner cast a withering glance at Mr. Clayton, and fiercely addressed him:

"So, Sir Yeoman, I have been informed that you are among those ill-disposed subjects of Her Majesty who dare to read the Bible, and forsooth, to understand its meaning, and to explain it to others in a way contrary to that which our Holy Mother the Church allows, and, therefore, contrary to the truth. How is it that you, a simple-minded man, who might better attend to your cattle and your swine, can venture to commit such folly?"

"My Lord Bishop, since you demand an answer, I will reply," said Clayton; with all the calmness he could command. "I am told, and believe, that the Bible is the Word of God, and in it I find that I am directed to search the Scriptures, and that if I do so, with prayer, that I shall have the guidance of God's Holy Spirit to enlighten my mind, and to enable me to understand them. This, and this alone, have I done."

"Ah! Knave, you acknowledge then that you have the right to set up your opinion against that of the Church and our Holy Father, the Pope?" exclaimed Bonner. "You are thus, me-thinks, a worse heretic than many who have gone to be burned, a fate which I doubt not will be yours unless you gain wisdom."

"My Lord Bishop, I crave your pardon, I trust not to my own opinion," said Reginald Clayton.

"Ah! I thought not," exclaimed Bonner, interrupting him. "Thou wilt be wise then, and recant."

"I said not that; but I was about to say that I put my trust in the Lord, and in His Word, and fear not what man can do unto me."

"That is to be seen, bold fellow," exclaimed Bonner. "Then thou dost not believe in Transubstantiation, Sir Knave?"

"I find not the matter explained in the New Testament," said Clayton humbly.

"Ah, ah! Nor, I warrant, in the effectiveness of penance and alms-giving?"

"I know the effectiveness, nay more, the necessity of repentance—a broken and a contrite spirit, and a firm trust in the one great sacrifice of our Lord Jesus Christ, whose blood alone can wash away sin," said Clayton, boldly; "I find no word of penance in the Scriptures, nor do I see that alms-giving can win Christ when He is won already by faith; yet I doubt not that alms-giving, if done for love of Him, is well-pleasing in His sight."

"Hold! Hold! Thou most disputative heretic," exclaimed the Bishop, with a fierce frown on his brow, "thou wilt have to bridle thy tongue the next time we meet, or to the stake you will go. Ho, warder, take this knave back to prison!"

Thus finished Reginald Clayton's mock examination. He was conducted back to prison as he came, in the company of others, who, not being wanted just then for burning, were allowed to drag on existence in its foul-smelling dungeons. There he and others remained for weeks, compelled to live with the vilest outcasts, and feed on the worst fare. Still he bore up manfully, and was not without consolation. Though he had not been allowed to bring his Bible, he remembered, and could repeat many, many passages, and often large portions, which brought joy and comfort to his soul, and instruction and often comfort likewise to those who listened. Some there for the first time heard the truths of the Gospel, the believing in which brought them joy, and peace, and life eternal.

He had another consolation in the trust that his children had escaped, and were in safety. This was at length confirmed by a note, which John Goodenough contrived to have conveyed to him, though John had to pay a heavy bribe to obtain his object.

After weeks of suffering, when, under like circumstances, the spirits of many had given way, he was once more conveyed into the presence of the Bishop. This time numerous persons were present, and among them, though in the dress of an ecclesiastic, he recognized Master Dixon, who, however, appeared to be utterly unconscious that they had ever before met.

On this occasion Bonner pushed home his questions with far more vehemence than before. On the first, he had seemed like a cat playing with her prey; now he looked as if prepared to rend his victim. "Thou are a most defiant and rebellious heretic," fiercely exclaimed the Bishop at length. "Had I required more evidence of your heresy, I possess it at hand, but I have enough and to spare to burn you ten times over! Away with him! And let him be taken to Smithfield, there to atone for his most abominable crimes at the stake! I will forthwith make out the order for his execution!"

Now, Reginald Clayton, you have need of all your resolution—of all your strength—of all your faith; for, to-morrow, you will have to endure ignominy, torture, and death; yet you cheerfully accept all, looking to that crown of glory in the heaven which fadeth not away!

Chapter 11

WHAT A DAY!

Humphrey Clayton had more difficulty in overcoming his sister's wish to return with him to London, than his uncle's objections to his going. Directly his strength was restored, in the peasant's disguise in which he had arrived, he set forth towards London on the pony on which his sister had journeyed to this place. He was seldom questioned, for few troubled themselves about the peasant youth, who was, those thought who took note of him, going to seek his fortune in the capital.

He was able also to pay for his food and lodging, for he had brought with him the store of gold pieces he had saved for the purchase of a Bible, which the good merchant had refused to receive from him. He could not, as before, sleep in the open air, for the year was advanced. November had commenced, and the nights were cold and damp.

Humphrey pushed onwards as fast as his pony could go, following the road he had come, so at length he found himself in the neighbourhood of honest Thomas Holden's cottage, towards which his pony set off at full speed. The door was closed. He knocked and knocked, but in vain. He looked in through the window. The interior had a deserted appearance; he thought perhaps that both Holden and his wife had left home for a short time together. He was still wandering round the cottage, when an old man, coming out of the wood passed him.

"What art thou looking for, lad?" asked the old man. Humphrey inquired if he knew what had become of the Holdens. "Ah, troth do I! They were carried away to London city, some time since, I wot not how long, to be burned, for the reason that they had sheltered two young heretics who had escaped out of the hand of the Lord Bishop Bonner!"

"Oh! Don't say that! Don't say that, old man, for the love of heaven!" exclaimed Humphrey. "Don't tell me that those kind, good people have been cruelly put to death on my account."

"Ah! Merry do I, though," said the old man in a well-satisfied tone; "if they were heretics, it is but right that they should be burned, and then they can do no more harm."

Sick at heart at what he had heard, Humphrey asked no further questions of the old man about his friends, but begged that the shortest way to London might be pointed out to him, and as soon as it was so, he set off towards the great city as fast as his pony could carry him. He felt that it was too probable, if the poor people like the Holdens were to be burned, his father would not escape.

Night overtook him before he reached the capital. Dark, however, as it was, he still, in his eagerness, pushed onwards until he became sensible that he had lost his way, for, looking up at the stars overhead, he found that he was almost turning back in the direction from which he had come.

The country was wild and hilly, and at length, as he led on his pony, he stumbled into a pit, from whence gravel had been taken to form the road. It was shallow and free from water, and it was thus completely sheltered from the wind, and somewhat also from the dew, by the high overhanging bank that had been hollowed out. He made up his mind to remain where he was, lest he should get into greater trouble. There he lay, holding his pony by the bridle, for he thought if the animal strayed he might not be able again to find it.

The long November night passed wearily away. His intention was to go to Newgate, and to seek an interview with his father in the character of a poor boy on his estate; then, if he was not detained, to endeavor to find out where the Holdens were confined.

Should they have escaped death, he purposed offering to deliver up himself in their stead, so that they would be allowed to go free. "I shall not be recognized," he thought to himself, "and I will say that I bear a message from young Humphrey Clayton, who would rather meet death than allow others to suffer for helping him." Having arrived at this resolution, he at length fell asleep.

The dawn had already broken when he awoke refreshed, and with a lightness of heart for which he could not account. It was the 17th of November 1558—a day to be remembered in the annals of England's history. In a short time he saw before him, in the far distance, the tower of St. Paul's Church, though a very different edifice to that afterwards raised on the same spot. With the tower as his guide, which rose above the generally low and mean houses that intervened, he, without difficulty, directed his course towards London.

As he got near the houses, he saw a number of people emerging from them, and hurrying in the direction of a spot he remembered too well. It was Smithfield. At first his tongue refused to ask the reason why they were thus hurrying on. At length he mustered courage, though trembling to hear the answer—

"Why, master, to see the chiefest sight we have had there for some weeks past. A whole batch of heretics are to be burned this morning, most defiant knaves, they say; and some women, too. O lad, it will be a pleasant and joyous sight; all for the honour of our holy religion, and the Queen, and Pope, and Cardinal Legate," answered a savage and rough-looking fellow, who seemed scarcely willing to stop and speak, lest he might miss any part of the expected spectacle.

Such men existed then, and ever since have been found, increased unhappily in numbers, in England's metropolis.

Humphrey, sick at heart and trembling with anxiety, followed as fast as he could make his way through the crowd.

The mass of people grew denser and denser as he approached the spot. There were many others on horseback; but with his little pony he was able to work his way towards the front, so as to look over the heads of all intervening spectators.

In the centre of the open space, where the ground was black with the ashes of previous fires, were eight or more stakes, with a pile of faggots surrounding each of them; beyond was a group of persons, ecclesiastics by their dresses; and justices, as the magistrates were called; and guards; others who were evidently prisoners.

Humphrey would have rather deserted his little pony than not have gone forward, yet he could not venture to approach the group on horseback. Among the crowd he observed a boy whose countenance pleased him.

"Here, lad, I will give thee a silver crown if thou wilt take charge of this animal and restore him to me when I return," he said.

He threw the reins to the boy, and pushed his way through the crowd. Regardless of the consequences, he rapidly shouldered his way onwards, for among the prisoners, he had recognized his father! There were others also— Thomas Holden and his wife. He was too late, he feared, to put into effect his resolution of offering himself instead of them. If he could not rescue his father, he would have the satisfaction of embracing him again, of being with him to the last.

Priests surrounded each prisoner, exhorting him to recant. They pointed to the stakes and faggots, and promised liberty, and restoration to home and family. The prisoners, one and all, refused the proffered pardon, and smiled at the stakes and faggots.

Humphrey, unable to resist the impulse of his heart, in spite of priests and guards, rushed forward, and threw himself on his father's neck.

"Who is that lad, who dares to impede the ministration of the priests to the condemned HERETIC?

Remove him, guards," said one of the principal of the ecclesiastics.

Humphrey, for an instant, looked up. In the speaker he recognized Master Dixon, their treacherous visitor at the farm. Disregarding him, and the soldiers who pressed around:

"Father, dear father, I will rescue you from these people, or die with you. There are many in the crowd who would aid us in a bold attempt at escape."

"Think not of it, my boy," answered Reginald Clayton in a firm tone. "Your own life would be sacrificed and I should not preserve mine. Fly, rather, at once, and be a support and protection to your sister. I grieve that you have come here; yet you did it through your love for me, and I bless you—Go, son, go. These are my last commands, and wherever you go, hold fast to the truth."

With a sad heart Humphrey was about to obey, when the priest who had called himself Master Dixon shouted out—

"Hold fast that youth, an arrant young heretic. By St. Nicholas, he shall burn with his father. Haste, pile up the faggots; let the broiling begin."

Scarcely were the words out of his mouth when there was a swaying to and fro of the crowd in the distance, and a horseman appeared, spurring at full speed towards where the priests and executioners were collected near the prisoners. It was evident that he brought news of importance.

"News! News!" he shouted. *"Queen Mary is dead! Elizabeth now reigns as Queen of England!"*

"Long live Queen Elizabeth, the Protestant Sovereign of England," cried a loud voice from the crowd.

"True it is, friends," exclaimed the horseman. "And, moreover, Sir William Cecil, a staunch Protestant, has been called to be Her Majesty's first minister. What that means you may all judge."

On hearing these words, the priests, who had just before appeared so proud and overbearing, turned pale, and began to whisper among themselves. The chief magistrate, who had been presiding at the fearful ceremony, sidled out from among them, two or three other officials, the executioners, moved off more rapidly, and quickly disappeared.

The debased ruffians whose business it was to heap up the faggots stood gaping at each other, and at their expected victims, and from them to their superiors, doubtful when they were to begin their work. The guard who had seized Humphrey let him go. Humphrey instantly flew back to his father, and throwing himself in his arms, exclaimed—

"There is hope, there is hope! Oh, father, there is hope!"

Yes, there was hope; for already the evil and cowardly priests and magistrates, who had been so eager to shed the blood of their fellow-creatures, began to tremble for their own lives. The chief magistrate at length stood up, and in a faltering voice cried out, "Lieges, it seemeth to me that matters are in an uncertain, doubtful condition, and, albeit these people deserve to die, it seemeth wise that they should be remanded forthwith to prison."

Not any official or priest opposed the proposition. Some few of the mob grumbled at being disappointed of their expected entertainment, but the great mass threw up their caps, and shouted lustily, "Long live Queen Elizabeth!"

Reginald Clayton, released from his bonds, passed his hand over his brow, like one awakening out of a sleep, and leaning on the arms of his faithful son, walked amid the guards back towards the prison from which he had that morning been led forth, as he believed, to die.

He and his companions, however, scarcely looked like the people going to prison, for they had assuredly a strong hope of speedy deliverance. Humphrey would gladly have shared his father's imprisonment, but at the door he was refused admittance. He was, however, able to supply him with some gold pieces, which, even in prison in those days, enabled him to obtain the share of a room with a few other gentlemen, and better food than the ordinary prison fare.

Among the last in the train of prisoners came honest Thomas Holden and his wife. Humphrey, after parting with his father, had time to run back and meet them. He pressed a piece of gold into Thomas's hard palm as he grasped it.

"No, lad, no; take back thy money," said the sturdy yeoman; "I thank thee kindly, but those who put us into this place shall even feed us while they keep us; and, when we get out, our own legs are strong enough to carry us home again, I ween."

Nothing Humphrey could urge would turn honest Thomas from his resolution.

When, finally, the prison doors were closed, Humphrey remembered his pony, which he had left with a boy in Smithfield, and he turned back, little expecting however, to find it. Just as he reached the precincts of the spot, still so full of dreadful recollections, he heard a voice, in melancholy accents, calling his name, and the next instant he found himself in the embrace of John Goodenough, who could scarcely speak for the sighs and groans which burst from his bosom, and the tears streaming from his eyes.

"It's too late—too late—it's all over; every one of them are burned, and the fires are nearly out, and the people gone," he exclaimed, giving way to a fresh burst of grief.

Not without difficulty, Humphrey made him comprehend what had occurred, and that his father was still alive and well. John had only just before arrived on the spot from Essex, where he had but that morning received the information that his master was to be put to death that day. His deep grief was soon turned into intense joy when he heard that Queen Elizabeth, known to be a Protestant, had ascended the throne. It was soon discovered how he had been mistaken. When the greater number of the crowd had dispersed, a few of the rougher characters, not altogether to be disappointed of their intended spectacle, had seized on the faggots left by the frightened executioners, and had made bonfires of them, in honour of the new Queen of England.

On advancing a short distance further, Humphrey espied his pony still held by the honest lad to whose charge he had committed him. Humphrey thanked him warmly, and rewarded him with a far larger piece of money than he had promised. The lad looked wistfully at him as he was going away. Humphrey, turning back, asked if he could do anything for him.

"Indeed, indeed you can, for I realize that you are a gentleman, in spite of your disguise. My parents are both dead, and I have no relations on whom to depend. Take me into your service, and I will prove truly faithful."

Humphrey consulted with John Goodenough, and then, turning to the lad, asked if he could ride.

"Ay, that I can," he answered, "I have lived all my days in the country, and travelled, too, over many a long mile of it!"

"Then will you undertake to bear a message for me into Wiltshire with all speed?" asked Humphrey.

The lad, who said that his name was Stephen Mason, finally undertook to make the best of his way to the house of William Fuller, with the news of the ascension of Queen Elizabeth, and the happy escape from death of Humphrey's father; and Humphrey resolved to appeal to the Queen should his father not soon be released, while John hurried back into Essex to prepare, as he hoped, for his dear master's return home. He was not disappointed. On the 24th of November, Queen Elizabeth made her public entrance into London, winning all the hearts of the people by her gracious and kind manners and courteous speeches. She also won their hearts by the order she forthwith issued that, in further honour of that day, all prisoners confined on account of their religious opinions should be forthwith set at liberty.

Throughout London the prison doors were thrown open; and those who had been till lately expecting death went forth to rejoice. To those who valued the Bible, an act of her Majesty on a similar occasion, a few weeks afterwards, gave still further satisfaction. When she viewed a pageant at the little Conduit in Cheape, she demanded what should be represented therein. Answer was made that Time did then attend for her.

"Time?" said she; "how is that possible seeing that it is Time that hath brought me hither?" A valuable lesson to all men to wait patiently for whatever God in His wisdom has in store for us. Here a Bible in English, richly covered, was let down unto her by a silk lace from a child that represented Truth. She kissed both her hands—with both her hands she received it—then she kissed it, afterwards applied it to her breast, and lastly, held it up, thanking the city especially for that gift, and promising to be a diligent reader thereof.

Humphrey was at the door of the prison to receive his father, with faithful John Goodenough holding their horses, and a crowd of friends eager to welcome those who had escaped, as it were, from the very jaws of death. A joyous company rode back into Essex, for many had been brought out of the county, ready to suffer at the stake rather than abandon their faith in the Gospel.

In a few days Mary arrived at her home, escorted by her uncle, who came to congratulate his brother-in-law on his happy escape from a cruel death. Together they visited the spot in Brentwood where Humphrey and Mary had witnessed the martyrdom of William Hunter—the cause of their own conversion to the truth, and of many others. "Truly," they said, "he did not die in vain!" "No!" And while the names of the sheriffs, the justices, the priests, the guards, and the whole of that multitude we found collected at the beginning of our tale watching his death, have long since been utterly forgotten, that of the young martyr is still cherished in his native town, and known throughout the world.

A monument of polished granite stands near the spot where his frail body perished, and the glorious cause for which he suffered, the free circulation of the Bible, which tells us of the love of God for man; the truth, as it is in Christ Jesus, is triumphant!